Miss Gargoyle smiled to herself, then, reaching up to the white roses, she plucked something from them and put it into her mouth. She chewed slowly, and with obvious enjoyment. Having swallowed loudly, she went into the lodge and closed the door behind her.

'Oh, oh,' moaned Harry, grabbing at his stomach and writhing. 'Did you see what she did? Oh, how awful! Dreadful!'

Polly felt quite sick.

'Disgusting,' she agreed in a weak voice.

'A caterpillar!' said Harry hoarsely. 'She ate a caterpillar – all green and wiggly, and she ate it. Oh, yuk, YUK!'

When Polly arrives at The Shrubbery to stay with her relatives, she soon discovers that something very sinister indeed is going on. Where are her two uncles? And what is the secret surrounding Miss Gargoyle, the strangest gardener Polly has ever seen . . .?

REBECCA LISLE

Shrubbery Skulduggery

YEARLING BOOKS

For June Lisle

SHRUBBERY SKULDUGGERY

A YEARLING BOOK 0 440 86277 9

First published in Great Britain by Doubleday, a division of
Transworld Publishers Ltd

PRINTING HISTORY
Doubleday edition published 1990
Yearling edition published 1992

Yearling Books are published by Transworld Publishers Ltd.,
61–63 Uxbridge Road, Ealing, London W5 5SA, in Australia by
Transworld Publishers (Australia) Pty. Ltd., 15–23 Helles Avenue,
Moorebank, NSW 2170, and in New Zealand by Transworld Publishers
(N.Z.) Ltd., 3 William Pickering Drive, Albany, Auckland.

Printed and bound in Great Britain by
Cox & Wyman Ltd., Reading, Berks.

Chapter One

'I *hate* birds!' Polly said, picking up a stray feather from the sofa and dropping it into the wastepaper bin. 'I hate them.'

She stomped wearily round the room, frowning at the framed pictures of parrots, thrushes, toucans and other birds that covered the walls. 'And I hate *feathers*, and *beaks*, and *eggs*, and birds' *legs* and birds' *claws* . . . and now, now, I hate South America.'

'Nonsense, dear,' said her father mildly, not even pausing from rummaging in the desk drawer.

'Yes I do . . . particularly South America. I just can't see why you need to go there at all.'

'Because of the birds, Polly. I told you, it's a chance in a lifetime to go there and study them.'

'But,' said Polly, 'I thought you knew everything there was to know about every bird in the whole world, anyway.'

'Did you, Polly? How nice. Isn't that nice, Margaret,' he said to his wife, 'to have such an admiring daughter?'

'And you do, don't you?' Polly went on. 'So why do you have to go?'

Her father turned back to the drawer and pulled out some more papers. He appeared not to have heard her and yet she knew he had.

'That letter must be here somewhere,' he muttered, showering paperclips, a half-eaten lollipop, an empty ink cartridge and some bird seed on to the floor. 'I'm amazed I still can't remember the number.'

'I'd be amazed if you did,' said Polly's mother. 'If only you would just *sometimes* file things.'

She was sitting painting at a very neat, well-ordered table. The brushes were arranged according to size and texture in clean jars; tubes of paint lay in rows – all with their caps on – and somehow, she had managed to still keep one jar of water clean. On her drawing board was a beautiful picture of a baby parrot, all reds and greens. She didn't look up as she spoke, but shook her head gently.

'Oh, Mummy, please. I don't want to be

sent away to this Shrubbery place where Daddy's family live. I want to come to South America with you. Say I can, please!'

'You know that's not possible, Polly dear.'

'Here it is!' Polly's father cried joyfully, waving a crumpled, grubby letter which he had pulled from the depths of the drawer. 'Good Lord! Dated three years ago. Doesn't time fly! I really should keep in touch with the family a little more often.'

'They don't exactly phone every week,' said Margaret.

'No, darling, but . . .'

'You know, Polly, we've tried everyone else,' she said, and this time she put down her brush and looked at her daughter. 'Darling, you know we have. The news of this trip came so suddenly; there isn't anyone else who could take you at such short notice except them – they never go away and they're relations, they can't refuse . . . We haven't any choice. Besides,' she added, 'I think it will be a good thing to see Daddy's family.'

'Why? *You* don't see them!'

'Polly . . . ! Anyway, as I said, we haven't any choice.'

'You could choose not to go,' said Polly, feeling mean. Her mother's troubled frown stopped her from saying anything meaner and, instead, she suggested for the hundredth time: 'Or, I could come with you.'

'Not suitable,' said her father, who hadn't

appeared to be listening, but as usual had managed to hear what Polly hadn't wanted him to and not what she *had* wanted him to. 'Jungles are not suitable for little girls of nine.'

'Ten, actually.'

'Even less for girls of ten.'

He picked up the telephone and began dialling a long number. 'Now, shush, I'm going to phone them to fix the details.'

'Your father's relations are nice,' said Polly's mother vaguely. She leaned back, narrowing her eyes to stare at her picture. 'Do you think this parrot looks cross-eyed? He looks as if he's squinting at that grape, doesn't he? I knew I'd put his eyes too close together . . . They'll look after you splendidly and the garden's wonderful. They don't bear *you* any grudge anyway, dear. Why, they said in their last letter how delighted they'd be to see you any holiday, and that cousin Harry was just about your age too.'

'That was three years ago,' moaned Polly.

'Which doesn't mean Harry will have stopped growing,' growled her father.

'But they might not want me now,' said Polly. 'If you haven't written in three years . . . They're probably busy. Oh, please . . . not people I've never met, not for the whole summer. I want to see South America and – what's it called? – "broaden my horizons". Please!'

'Nonsense,' said her father. 'Anyway, The Shrubbery will broaden your horizons for you. You know nothing about plants . . . Oh, here we go . . . Hello? Hello, is that The Shrubbery? Kitty? Hello, this is Edward. *Edward*, your brother . . .'

Chapter Two

The train station was chilly. Polly's father stamped his feet and shuffled them impatiently as he scanned the end of the line for the train.

'I don't want to go, Daddy.'

'Not again, Polly! It's too late now, you're going to The Shrubbery and that's that. You'll have a super time. Oh, look, here's the train.'

'Perhaps it's the wrong one?'

'It's the right one.'

'If I did come to South America with you,' said Polly, 'I could help by climbing up the trees to look in the nests and I could mix Mummy's colours for her and squeeze out the paints . . . Gosh, really, I don't know how you'll manage without me!'

But her words were drowned by the wheeze and roar of the train as it rumbled towards them along the station. It drew slowly to a halt with a loud screech of brakes.

Polly's father peered through the train windows. 'Ah, good,' he said, spotting a compartment with just an elderly woman in the far corner, 'this one will do nicely. In you go, sweetheart.'

Polly gazed up at her father with one last hurt expression, but it wasn't any good, he didn't even see it. She climbed into the window seat while her father stacked her bags in the rack above.

'Bye-bye, dear,' he said, patting her on the head and giving her a kiss. 'Send them our love and . . . Oh, this is for you,' he added, passing her a large wicker basket. 'A little surprise present for being so good about it all. And take this too, will you.' He handed her a long, tubular cardboard box. 'There's a plant inside. It's for my sisters, but don't give it to them straightaway. Wait until it flowers . . . Are you concentrating, Polly? I said, wait until the buds open and then give it to them. It's very delicate and special so I want you to water it every day and keep it in the sun. Tell them . . . Oh, never mind, it's too late now. Be good and helpful, there's my pretty Polly.'

Before she could say another word, her father

had slammed the door shut and a whistle blowing loudly nearby drowned the last words of advice on plant care and good behaviour that he tried to give her.

Noisily, the train began to pull out of the station, and Polly leaned out of the window in the door and waved.

She was glad to see that long after there was any point in standing on the platform, she could still make out the little red dot of her father's duffel coat as he stood all alone on the deserted station, waving to the disappearing train.

When that last familiar sight had passed from view, she closed the window and went back into the compartment.

She slumped down in her seat. Huh! Pretty Polly! Pretty Polly! she thought crossly. I'm not a rotten parrot, I'm a girl! Her father, she thought, sometimes mixed these facts up.

The large woman in the far corner smiled kindly at her and Polly smiled back. She hoped she wouldn't want to talk; women who wore the sort of hat this woman wore - like a squashed pink marshmallow - always talked about their grandchildren, television programmes and knitting, and Polly wasn't interested in any of these topics. Besides, she wanted to look out of the window and think.

The town sped past and was soon replaced by green fields interwoven with hedges and fences and round hills covered in dark patches of trees. She liked the countryside. Polly's thoughts rushed ahead of the train to The Shrubbery, where she was going to stay with her relatives. In the last couple of days she had learnt a lot about these relations. Before, she had only known, vaguely, that they existed at all.

There were three aunts: Kitty, Constance and Winifred, all her father's sisters, and two uncles whose names she couldn't remember who were married to the two younger aunts. And then there was the cousin, Harry. They all lived in a big old house called The Shrubbery and were all gardeners, or horticulturists, which meant they knew a great deal about plants instead of birds. It was extraordinary, thought Polly, seeing they were the same family, that her cousin was not called Dandelion or Tulip or even Petal. But then he was a boy. And probably *his* parents didn't let their work and lives get so mixed up: her mother had poured out a packet of wild bird food into her bowl only that morning thinking it was muesli.

Cousin Harry . . . I bet he's awful, she thought. He'll have straw in his hair and talk about pigs all the time or else grass and new breeds of cacti. It's not fair! My life is ruined. I'll never forgive my parents, never!

Polly's dark, gloomy thoughts were so absorbing that it was several seconds before she realized the woman in the corner was talking to her.

'Excuse me! Excuse me, little girl.'

'Yes? Sorry,' said Polly, 'I was miles away.'

'I'm going to get some lunch from the

buffet car. I just wondered if I could get you something,' said the woman.

'Thank you,' said Polly, 'but I've got a packed lunch.'

'All right, dear. Just thought I'd ask. If they're doing something cooked, I might stay, but otherwise I'll be straight back. You'll be all right on your own?'

'Oh, yes.'

'See you in a minute then.' The plump woman squeezed out of the compartment and disappeared down the corridor.

As soon as she had gone, Polly heaved a sigh of relief: she much preferred to be on her own and now she could have her sandwiches without worrying about having to share them. She had just got the packet out of her bag when a strange noise suddenly broke the quiet.

Polly looked around. She couldn't see anything but it sounded very close - right beside her, in fact.

She listened carefully: it was a snappy sound and yet it wasn't mechanical, more animal-like. She looked about suspiciously; there wasn't anything there. Quickly she swung her feet up so they weren't dangling over the edge of the seat - whatever it was could be right beneath her!

16

There it was again! The noise grew louder and louder and it was now accompanied by a rustling and scratching. Suddenly she realized where it came from: it was the present her father had given her – the large wicker basket on the seat beside her.

Gingerly, she undid the latch.

The moment the catch was undone, the lid sprang back and a mass of yellow and turquoise feathers exploded out of the basket accompanied by a tremendous cry of 'Yark! Yark!' The bird, for it had to be one, sounded very cross. It fluffed its feathers and made snapping noises. The shape began to sort itself out: two wings were preened into order and a long tail laid out over the back of the basket.

It was a large tropical bird.

'Yark? Ark?' said the bird more softly, looking at Polly with its beady, bright eyes.

'Oh, yuk!' said Polly, unkindly. 'A rotten old parrot!'

'Pretty Polly! Pretty Polly!' squawked the bird. 'No need to be rude!'

'But our home's full of birds,' said Polly. 'Mummy paints them and Daddy studies them: trust him to imagine you'd be a surprise! Honestly, they don't know anything!'

'And you don't know anything either,' said
the bird, 'if you think I'm a parrot. I thought *you*
would recognize a macaw when you saw one,
especially the Supreme Champion of Champion
Macaws!'

'What?'

'The Supreme Champion of Champion Macaws . . . and you mean "pardon".'

'Did you say that?' asked Polly, wide-eyed
with amazement.

18

'No,' said the macaw, 'it was the basket.'

'Oh, it *was* you!'

'Very observant,' said the bird. 'Very quick on the uptake, I must say.'

'Did Daddy teach you?'

'He taught me to say "Pretty Polly". I taught myself the art of polite conversation! Ha, ha, ha!' And he laughed: a noise like an old lawnmower dragging over cobblestones. Polly shivered.

'What are you called?'

'Well, it could be Joey. Or even Polly.'

'Hmm. Those wouldn't suit you. I'm going to call you Morris.'

'Morris, eh? Not bad, not bad at all.' He nodded his head and strutted up and down the basket. 'I could grow to like that,' he said. 'By the way, was that the rustle of crisps and sandwich packaging I just heard? I resisted the temptation to meet that granny with the pink meringue on her head, but I would find it very hard to resist a peanut butter sandwich.'

'What made you think they were peanut butter?' asked Polly.

'Superb sense of smell, A1 vision and wishful thinking,' said the bird. 'Please tell me I'm right.'

'You're right,' said Polly, breaking the

sandwiches in half. 'Here you are.'

They shared Polly's lunch and when Morris had finally pecked every scrap from the apple core, he walked up the seat to the luggage rack, where, after muttering softly for a while, he went to sleep. The long conversation, after so many weeks of 'Pretty Polly', had quite worn him out.

When Polly's other travelling companion came back, she was so full of her cooked lunch that she didn't even notice Morris. She smiled at Polly, then went on to describe in detail precisely what she had eaten, before she fell asleep, leaving the compartment quiet and peaceful for several hours.

Sometime in the afternoon, the train stopped at a station and when Polly looked out, she saw a big banner strung up between two trees which said: POLLY GET OFF THE TRAIN. So she thought she better had.

She put Morris back in the hamper and the elderly woman helped her to get down her bags and put them on the platform.

'Someone coming to meet you, dear?' asked the woman. 'It looks a funny sort of place to me.'

'That's because they're a funny sort of person,' said Polly, confidently. 'Family, you know. Someone will come, I'm sure.'

Polly waved as the train disappeared again. It had been easy to sound brave on the train, but now it had gone she had to admit she was rather nervous. There was no going back now.

It was only a tiny station, with no ticket collector or waiting-room. In fact, there was no one in sight at all. Polly was just beginning to wonder if she'd been forgotten, when a tall, tweed-suited woman appeared through a gate and made towards her.

'Hello there!' she cried. 'Polly? Yes, thought it must be. I'm your Aunt Winifred. How d'you do?' and she pumped Polly's hand up and down vigorously.

'How do you do?' said Polly.

Polly's aunt wore thick woolly stockings and sensible shoes. Perched on her head was an alpine hat with a green feather in it. This is even worse than I expected, Polly thought. I'm going to be made to go hiking, eat the crusts and be healthy. Ugh!

'Come along then,' said Aunt Winifred, picking up Polly's bags. 'This way!' And she strode off, swinging the bags so effortlessly they might have been empty.

'What's in here?' she asked, indicating the hamper.

'A bird. A macaw, actually. Daddy gave it to me.'

'We don't have any birds ourselves. Watch the cats don't get him!'

'Yark!' came a troubled cry of agreement from the basket.

'I will,' said Polly, almost running to keep up with her aunt. 'Wasn't it nice of the station master to let you put up that notice for me?' she added, rather breathlessly. 'What a good idea!'

'What station master?' said Aunt Winifred. 'There's no station master here.'

'Oh, who looks after the station then?'

'What station?'

'The one the train stopped at.'

'That's not a station. That's the bottom of the garden. The train just happens to pass this way. It stopped by arrangement.'

'You must have an enormous garden,' gasped Polly.

'We have.'

Her aunt didn't speak again, but kept her chin high and her eyes straight ahead, so Polly didn't dare ask any more questions. Besides, there were

lots of interesting things to look at.

They were walking down a path which curved and plunged through the vegetation like the big dipper at the fair, and all around were plants of every size and description.

There were giant trees with peeling bark and thin trees with striped bark, a tree with a twisted trunk like barley sugar and a tree almost lying on the ground, its branches sweeping the grass. There were vast bushes covered with yellow flowers, rhododendrons with shiny rubbery leaves, spiky tropical-looking flowers, and ordinary-looking daisies and roses. Whichever direction Polly looked, she could see only plants and more plants, stretches of grass or neat box hedges. Many of the plants were labelled with their botanical names, but Aunt Winifred was going too fast for Polly to get a chance to read them.

They were following one of the many tiny paths which zigzagged through the undergrowth. These tracks were signposted to exciting places like: THE MARBLE FOUNTAIN, THE SWEET PEA COLLECTION, THE MAZE. And less exciting ones like: WHEELBARROWS, POTTING SHEDS and THE HOUSE.

After a while, Polly caught sight of the roof

of a large building through the trees and, a little later, the path widened out in front of a lawn and she found herself looking across a vast expanse of emerald green to the house itself.

The Shrubbery was very old and had been subjected to many people's different ideas of architecture. As a result it was a mixture of towers and battlements, steep roofs and flat roofs, terraces and balconies. Of all the many windows of different shapes and sizes, Polly guessed that no two were alike.

'It's lovely!' she gasped.

'It's The Shrubbery,' said her aunt. 'Our home and our place of work.'

They walked across the springy grass to the large front door, and Polly noticed, as they drew nearer, that at each window rows of plant pots or else windowboxes overflowed with brilliant, colourful flowers. Clinging to the pale yellow walls of the house were vines, ivies, white and pink roses and purple-flowered clematis. It was as if the whole building was made of plants and was somehow a continuation of the wonderful garden around it: a living, breathing house.

'It's magical,' said Polly, gazing at it with amazement. 'The most wonderful house I've ever seen!'

Chapter Three

As they walked up the wide stone steps, the front door was thrown open and a friendly-looking woman ran down towards them. She had long hair and was younger than Aunt Winifred.

'Polly!' she cried. 'My dear little niece! How lovely to see you at last.' She threw her arms round Polly and kissed her loudly on both cheeks. 'I'm Kitty,' she said, beaming at Polly through her big round glasses and straightening her dishevelled hair. 'I haven't seen you since you were, oh, just a tiny little thing! You've grown. That was after Edward, your father, had left, of course,' she added.

'Did he live here then?' asked Polly, surprised.

'Of course. When he was a little boy he did,' she said, ushering Polly up the stairs, 'and later, but, well, gardening wasn't what he really wanted.'

'No, it's birds,' said Polly.

'Yes, birds. And he's doing well, isn't he? South America now, hmm? Wonderful!' But she looked rather wistful as she spoke. 'Come in, do come in, I shouldn't keep you here talking.'

Aunt Kitty helped Winifred to carry the bags up the steps and into the huge, stone-flagged hall.

'I have to get back to my sweet peas,' said Aunt Winifred. 'There's some labelling to finish. I won't be long. Will you give Polly some tea?'

Aunt Kitty nodded. 'Of course I will. Don't tire yourself, Winifred . . . we've a busy evening ahead. See you later.'

Polly was gazing round the hall in amazement. She had only seen places like this in the stately homes she'd visited or in books.

There was a wide staircase with twisted wooden banisters which swept upwards into an overhanging, crooked landing. By craning her neck she could see a high, domed ceiling with glass panels which let in a soft, natural light. Dark ancestral portraits decorated the walls: shivers rippled up Polly's spine when she thought that perhaps some of them were also related to her.

The air was heavy with the scent of flowers: roses, daisies, phlox, lavender and many others were arranged in jars around the hall. The perfume overflowed into the warm afternoon air, making it heavy and exotic.

'And this is Harry,' said Aunt Kitty, ushering forward a boy from the shadows. 'Your cousin.'

Polly jumped: she'd been in such a dream she hadn't even noticed him standing there. She managed to say hello, then peered at him anxiously, looking for the straw she'd been sure he'd be chewing.

The boy smiled at her through half-closed eyes and held out his hand. Polly wasn't used to shaking hands, especially not with other children and she gave him her hand reluctantly, then blushed crimson as he raised it to his lips.

'Charmed,' he said sweetly, then he made a great show of kissing his own hand loudly and dropping hers with a giggle.

'What a silly game,' said Aunt Kitty. 'Take no notice, Polly, we don't.' But Polly was so overcome with embarrassment that she couldn't even reply.

'Harry, take her bags up. The front tower room. Don't stand there like a nitwit, hurry up!'

Then Kitty led her down a short flight of stone steps to the kitchen. 'Are you hungry? What about something to eat?'

'No, I'm not really very hungry, thanks.'

'Sit yourself down. I'm sure I can find something to tempt you.'

Polly seated herself at the vast wooden table. Around her, copper pans gleamed in the early evening sunlight which streamed in through the open door. Outside, behind the house, Polly glimpsed neat rows of vegetables and lines of fruit trees. Two large dressers on either side of the room housed a vast collection of blue and white pots and, from the ceiling, dried herbs, cured meats and vast spoons hung like stalactites in a cave.

'This must be the nicest kitchen in the whole world,' said Polly.

'I sometimes think that too,' agreed Aunt Kitty, smiling.

Just then, Harry came in. He sat down at the great table beside Polly and scowled at her.

'Well, I never thought *you'd* come for a visit, Cousin,' he said.

'Why ever not?' asked Polly. 'I've been invited. Why shouldn't I come?'

'Don't you know? Can't you guess?' said Harry, mysteriously.

'No. I don't know what you're talking about.'

'Oh, do stop it, Harry. Stop teasing.'

'I don't care,' said Polly. 'Boys are naturally very childish at this age. I shan't lower myself to his infantile level.'

'Well done!' Aunt Kitty beamed at her; at the same time she hit her son playfully on the head with a big wooden spoon. 'Behave yourself! Now, Polly, you say you're not hungry, but I

think you might be tempted . . .'

Polly doubted it. She knew the sort of thing her other relation, her grandmother on her mother's side, cooked up for her as a special treat: tapioca pudding and coffee cake. No, thanks!

'Honestly,' Polly began, 'I'm really not . . .'

'You see,' Kitty went on, taking her glasses off and peering hard at her, 'you see, we've got a visitor for dinner tonight, so it would be better if you two have yours now. Down here in the kitchen.'

'What, *now*? Together?' roared Harry in disgust.

'Yes. That's what I said.'

'Rotten trick!' said Harry. 'We're not babies, you know.'

'Well, one of us isn't,' said Polly, coolly.

Harry glared at her.

'Our guest doesn't care much for children,' said Aunt Kitty, 'and we want to have a quiet talk. She can be a bit touchy.'

'So can I!' cried Harry.

'Of course it doesn't matter,' said Polly, hoping she sounded polite and grown-up, but inside she was upset. It'll be bread and butter, then up to bed, she thought. I'll never forgive my parents, never!

'Now,' said her aunt, putting on an apron. 'A cup of tea, or would you like to try some strawberry and banana milkshake – with ice-cream on top, of course.'

'Oh, milkshake, please!' they both cried, and when Polly caught Harry's eye, he smiled back. Perhaps he wasn't going to be *totally* dreadful, after all.

'Then you could have a little grilled cucumber; it's got cheese and eggs in it. Or one of these bacon and plum whirls? Or, how about one of these? She handed them a stuffed potato shaped like a little snowman, all covered in white sauce with a tiny carrot nose. 'I think these have turned out *most* successfully!'

'Wonderful!' agreed Polly. 'What a lot of cooking you've been doing!'

'Yes, haven't they! But who's special enough to deserve all this?' asked Harry. 'That's what I'd like to know.'

'Yes,' said Kitty.

'Yes, what?'

'Yes, she is special, in a special sort of way.'

'Oh, Mother!' Harry groaned, looking to the ceiling in dismay. 'Must you be so *vague*?'

'My father's just the same,' said Polly, biting eagerly into a parsnip coated with honey and baked to a crunchy crispness. 'It must run in the family.'

'And what a family!' agreed Harry.

'What's wrong with the others?'

'Wait till you meet them!' said Harry with a laugh.

'I'd like to meet them. Where are they all?' asked Polly. 'The other aunt and my uncles? Are they working in the garden or are they out?'

Aunt Kitty interrupted quickly before Harry could speak: 'Your uncles are away at a seed conference, we hope they'll be home soon.' She suddenly seemed to find it impossible to look directly at them, and quickly busied herself at the stove. 'They'll be home soon,' she repeated. 'It was a very important seed conference and of course they will have had to take notes and see people and things . . .' Her voice drifted off into a whisper and she stared blankly at a pan. 'All sorts of things could delay them, all sorts . . .'

'Well, I hope you're right,' said Harry. 'But I think it's all *very* odd . . . Anyway, Polly, the other aunt is Aunt Constance, and of course she's odd too. She hardly ever comes down here now. She's the oldest sister. She lives, eats and works upstairs in her room. She . . .'

'Finished?' It was Aunt Winifred, suddenly

bustling in from the garden.

'No!' the two children cried.

'Well, do hurry up.' Aunt Winifred peered over Kitty's shoulder. 'Everything all right? Think she'll like it?'

'Well *they* did,' said Aunt Kitty. 'I don't see how anyone couldn't appreciate it, really. Specially if they're, you know, *greedy* . . .'

'Good. I've finished doing my labels now, so I'll be able to help. All done, you two?' she added to the children. 'Good. Harry, I want you to show Polly round the garden – just a quick look – and then you're both to go to bed.'

'BED!' they both cried.

'You don't have to go to sleep. I know it's rather early,' said Aunt Winifred, 'but we can't have you two cluttering up the house when our guest comes, can we?'

'Can't we?'

'No, Harry!'

'You don't mind, do you, Polly?' said Aunt Kitty, hopefully. 'I am sorry about all this . . . we weren't expecting this, er, lady for dinner today, and what with the men away and everything, I don't feel as if you've had a proper welcome and I did want . . . And don't let Harry upset you. Any silly stories – well, just check them with me.'

Chapter Four

Harry led Polly outside.

At the back of the house was a walled section – the kitchen garden, which was sheltered and sunny and mild enough for delicate herbs to be grown all year round. Against the walls, pear, apple, and cherry trees were trained to grow in orderly, ladder-like patterns. From there, Harry led her through a gated archway which took them into the orchard where small, ball-shaped trees grew in tidy rows. Here were more apples, tiny golden pears and purple plums.

'Of course, we don't really go in for fruit,' said Harry. 'Flowering plants are our speciality, but since the trees are here, we make jams and chutney to sell. We haven't got a lot of helpers, so sometimes we're very overworked.'

'It's all lovely,' said Polly. 'I do envy you living here. I'd love it. And it's so big – I can hardly believe it . . .'

'Oh, yes, it's enormous!' said Harry. 'We've only time now for a quick look at the nearest bits. Holy hollyhocks! It would take about three weeks to see the whole lot properly.'

Polly felt this had to be a slight exaggeration, but thought it best not to comment.

'Come on, we'll go this way, past the monkey puzzle tree – do you know, it's one of the tallest in the whole county!'

They walked slowly along the path, Harry pointing out things of interest and Polly listening and occasionally asking questions.

'I'll just take you to that bridge,' said Harry, 'and then we'd better head back to the house. It's very silly wanting us to be in bed early like this, but I suppose we'd better try and do what they want. Mother's looking a bit weepy already and Aunt Winifred can be *dreadful* when she's angry.'

'But why are they both upset? Is it all the cooking? Don't you have guests for dinner very often?' asked Polly.

They had reached the bridge now, and they stopped to lean over its side and gaze down into the river below. The water was crystal clear and they could see several plump fish finning gently

in and out of the weeds.

'We hardly ever have guests,' said Harry. 'And this is the first time they've invited her!' He hit the stone wall crossly. 'Rotten Mother. Stick-in-the-mud Aunt Winifred. Fancy not telling me all about it.'

'About what?'

'About everything! They're worried sick because Dad and Uncle Fred haven't come back from this conference, and they won't admit it.'

'Have they phoned the police?'

'Of course not. You see, I think they know where they are.'

'What do you mean?'

'Want to know what I really think?'

'Yes.'

'Are you sure you can take it?'

'Try me.'

'Miss Gargoyle's got them. She's a new gardener here and boy, is she peculiar! Somehow, some way, she's at the bottom of all this.'

'You'll have to explain, Harry, I just don't understand.'

'OK. From the beginning then. This is a garden centre, right? Not an ordinary one, we don't let the public in often, we send the plants out - by post mostly. Haven't you heard of our *Shrubbery Selection Catalogue*?' Polly shook her head. 'We grow rare and wonderful plants. "Gorgeous gladioli", "beautiful begonias" - that's what it says in the brochure - and things you won't have heard of, like *Osteospermum jucundum* and *Carpenteria californica* . . .' He looked at her to check she was suitably impressed. Polly was. She wouldn't like to admit it, but she hadn't even heard of begonias.

'Well,' Harry continued, 'every now and

then, one of the grown-ups goes off to a conference about them. Two days ago it was a seed conference that Dad and Uncle Fred went to - WITH HER! And they never came back!'

'With this Miss Gargoyle?'

'Yes. And I overheard them talking earlier and that's who's coming tonight, the one and only Miss Gargoyle.'

He picked up a leaf and began shredding it into little pieces and dropping them over the bridge into the water.

'Nobody ever believes me. I told them right at the beginning that there was something peculiar about her, but they wouldn't listen. I can't imagine why they employed her - there are lots of good gardeners about who don't look so weird and don't behave so oddly . . . Do you know, when she thinks no one's looking, she steals fruit from the orchard and sneaks back to the lodge with it. Loads of it. She can't possibly eat it all, even though she's so fat! And why are they inviting her to dinner unless they're trying to butter her up? Unless they think she has something to do with Dad and Uncle Fred going off like this! They couldn't possibly just want to talk to her, they could do that any time. They don't even like her much.'

'But what on earth could she have done with two grown men?' asked Polly. 'And why would she want them? It sounds a bit crazy to me.'

'I have some ideas,' said Harry, 'but I can see you don't really believe me, just like everyone else, so what's the point in telling you? You don't believe *anything*.'

Polly couldn't argue. Would Harry believe her if she told him she had a talking macaw? She doubted it and yet it was true, and so, perhaps, was what he said.

The macaw! Morris!

'Oh, I've got to get back,' cried Polly. 'I forgot all about my poor bird. He's locked in the basket. He'll be hungry. Oh, poor Morris!'

'Brought a bird, have you? Can't see why people like birds: you can't prune them or pick them or anything . . . OK, come on, then,' said Harry, and he turned to go back to the house. 'You will believe me, though,' he added, as they walked along. 'If you're going to be a proper relative and a proper friend, you jolly well have to!'

By the time they reached the house, the shadows were lengthening and it was getting cooler. Polly was beginning to feel quite exhausted with all the new things she'd seen and heard: perhaps going to bed so early wasn't going to be such a bad idea.

Harry led her upstairs to her room.

'Hope you aren't easily scared,' he said. 'It's an old house and we've got lots of ghosts that come out when it's dark.'

'Oh, I like a bit of company at night,' said Polly, calmly.

Harry glanced at her sharply.

'You're not as bad as you look,' he said. And although this was far from polite, Polly found herself grinning as he showed her up the twisting staircase to her room.

She half expected her bedroom to be strewn with cobwebs, candle-lit and have no furniture from what Harry had said, but there was nothing sinister or frightening about it. In fact, it was delightful.

There were large french windows which led out on to a balcony, and the evening sun streamed in, making it light and pretty. It was completely circular so none of the furniture fitted neatly against the walls. It was quaint wooden furniture, painted pale blue and hand-decorated with flowers and bees. There was no carpet; a tiny bed stood on bleached floorboards, around which blue roses had been painted on a white border.

'Like it?'

'It's beautiful!'

'Aunt Constance used to have this room when she was a little girl. Bit soppy if you ask me,' said Harry, smiling.

'I like the flowers everywhere,' said Polly. 'Specially the roses, but there's no such thing as a blue rose, is there?'

They stared at the garlands of blue roses wreathed around the edge of the floor.

'No. Impossible. The nearest anyone's got is purple and they just look dirty. Aunt Constance painted them. Blue's her favourite colour. Well, good night then . . . Oh, the bathroom's down the hall, up two steps, turn right, down to the left, straight on past the big clock then it's the green door. OK? Good night. Sweet dreams!' And he was gone.

Quickly Polly rushed to open the wicker basket.

Morris was not pleased. He squawked loudly then climbed slowly out as if his legs were aching and uncomfortable. He unruffled his feathers slowly, clicking his beak crossly.

'Thanks for nothing!' he said. 'I suppose

you've had *your* tea? Pets should always come first, ever been told that? Dumb animals need care and attention.'

'But you're not dumb.'

'Huh!'

'I am truly sorry, Morris. I forgot, and then Harry was here and I didn't think you'd want to meet him.'

'I don't. I have no intention of speaking to anyone but you. And no, it won't happen again. You won't get me back in that basket again until we go home.'

He spread his crumpled wings, groaning heavily with each movement.

'I am sorry,' said Polly again.

'Good,' said Morris, not looking at her. He flapped slowly over to the bed as if in great pain, but Polly saw a flicker of a smile on his face and guessed, correctly, that he was exaggerating his complaints.

'Not a bad place,' he said, looking around. 'I do like to get away to the country, don't you?' And he flew through the window on to the balcony.

Polly ran out to join him and leaned over the railing to gaze down at the garden. The height made her dizzy: it was a very long way to the ground!

Below her the garden seemed to stretch for miles and miles. Far away something glinted in the evening sun: the railway line, she thought, and suddenly felt very homesick.

'Cheer up, Polly my old fruit,' said Morris. 'We're going to have fun here, I can tell. And lots of lovely dinners . . . Which reminds me

- you've had yours, so you won't mind if I fly off now, will you? There are some interesting-looking buzzing things about, and I did think I smelt some plums on the way in, but if you do see the odd grape, I would be *most* grateful . . . Bye-bye for now!' And he swooped down into the garden and was soon lost among the trees.

When he had quite disappeared, Polly unpacked her things.

She put the special plant her father had given her outside on the balcony where it would get the sun. It looked very healthy when she took it out of its container and there were several buds on it just ready to open, but it didn't look rare or in any way special to her.

She folded her T-shirts, jumpers and jeans neatly into the chest of drawers, but her best dress, pink scattered with embroidered hummingbirds, she scrunched into a ball and hid at the back of the bottom drawer. It was definitely not a pink hummingbird place, thank goodness. When that was finished she visited the bathroom, only losing her way twice, and was just thinking about getting undressed, although now she didn't feel tired at all, when there was a knock on the door.

'Hello?'

'It's me.' Harry's face appeared round the door. 'Want to come and do some detective work? Fancy spying on this mysterious dinner party?'

'Are you going to?'

'Certainly. Families should stick together. I don't like all these secrets.'

Polly thought for a moment. She ought to do as she was told and go to bed, particularly as she was a guest, but Harry looked so excited and would certainly be disappointed if she didn't go . . . It took her only a few moments to convince herself that it was, in fact, her duty to accompany him.

'OK,' she agreed. 'I'll come.'

Chapter Five

Downstairs, the hall was very dark and quiet.

They tiptoed past closed doors to the end of the passage, where light showed through the half-open dining-room door. As they drew near, they heard voices. Kneeling down in the shadowy corridor, they peeped in.

It took a few moments for Polly's eyes to adjust to the bright light, and then she began to take note of what she saw. Sitting at the head of the long dining table was an enormously fat woman with bright eyes and a most extra-ordinary amount of hair.

'I told you. See, I knew I was right,' Harry hissed in her ear.

'What? Is it her?'

'Yes. That's Miss Gargoyle.'

Miss Gargoyle was a gigantic woman. She seemed to ooze over the sides of her chair and spread, like rising dough, across the table. Her yellowish-green hair, elaborately styled, made her seem even larger. It was arranged very strangely: on the top, it was divided into plaits and coils, and these were wound round each other and piled up into three cone-shaped points. Thin ringlets hung like snakes over her shoulders and three long segments were draped over her back like strands of pale green seaweed. This mass of hair would have even looked remarkable at a royal gala, Polly thought, and here, beside Miss Gargoyle's gardening clothes – an old brown jumper, baggy brown trousers and wellington boots – it looked absolutely bizarre. She must have only just stopped work, Polly guessed, as propped behind the chair was a rake.

Miss Gargoyle did not have a very nice face, but Polly had been brought up never to judge people on the way they looked, so she tried to believe that she was actually quite pleasant. She was much older than the hairstyle suggested, at least forty, Polly thought, and her horrid, sneery expression did nothing to improve her appearance.

In front of Miss Gargoyle the laden dining table stretched out like an illustration for a party dinner in a cookery book: every type of pie, every colour of sauce, every shape of pudding and pastry, cake and custard was there. Silver cutlery gleamed against the crisp white cloth and

a glass of rich red wine glowed in a tall glass. But strangely, there was only one place laid, and only one glass – both in front of Miss Gargoyle.

There was an extraordinary look in Miss Gargoyle's eyes. Polly had seen that look before: it was the same look that Emma Williams next door had got when Polly showed her her new bike. It was the same expression that she had seen in her mother's eyes when she opened a new box of paints. It was a mixture of delighted anticipation and, in Miss Gargoyle's case, also greed!

Miss Gargoyle was scanning the dining table, looking intently at the food. So clearly was she imagining the tastes and textures of all the delicacies that she couldn't resist licking her lips and leaning forward like some ravenous animal.

Polly tried to be fair, but it was no good, she didn't like the look of the woman and the more she watched her, the surer she was that Harry's suspicions were correct.

Polly's amazement began to subside and she became aware that there were voices: Aunt Winifred and Aunt Kitty were both in the room too.

'Well, Miss Gargoyle, we're delighted you could come,' said Aunt Kitty. 'I hope you enjoy dinner. We know how you appreciate your food.'

'It is true I'm a gourmet,' said Miss Gargoyle. 'I do like a bit of haute cuisine.'

'In other words, she's as greedy as a pig!' Harry translated into Polly's ear.

'Do try this stuffed beetroot. How about these – cauliflower pancakes with bean and parsley sauce? Sausages in aspic? Curried aubergine with coconut and banana cream? Delicious, all of them!'

Miss Gargoyle, having contemplated the food for some time now, began to eat it as quickly as she could. She had a gigantic appetite, to match her gigantic size, and the food began to disappear with remarkable speed.

'Talk about greed!' hissed Harry.

'She really takes the biscuit!' Polly agreed, which made Harry choke so badly with laughter that for a moment they thought they'd be discovered.

'Must be the cat,' said Aunt Kitty, glancing suspiciously towards the door. 'She's been a bit off-colour recently.'

Miss Gargoyle spoke very little – she was too busy.

She ploughed her way rapidly through all

the savoury dishes, then, rather more slowly, started the puddings. A delicious chocolate soufflé with apricot sauce, peach and almond buns made into little pig shapes, yellow and pink striped blancmange, caramel sorbet covered in rum-soaked strawberries, and finally, meringue swans stuffed with tropical fruit, floating on a lake of ice-cream.

She ate it all.

At last, putting down her spoon and leaning back in her chair, she let out a volcanic belch.

'BUURP! Hmmm, very tast . . .'

'Oh, good, you *liked* it!' Aunty Kitty interrupted. 'Thank goodness!'

'No, no. I meant NASTY,' said Miss Gargoyle, hastily. 'Very nasty.'

'I don't believe you. You're just being difficult,' snapped Aunt Winifred. 'It was superb!'

'Yes, it really was,' said Aunt Kitty, 'so . . .'

'So what?'

'Now come on, Miss Gargoyle, you did suggest . . .'

'I never *suggest* anything.'

'You certainly did! You hinted that you knew something about Fred and Tom's disappearance and that a good meal might jog your memory. Quality food is good for the brain – those were your exact words! Well, you've had the meal, so what about it?'

'Don't shout, Winifred,' said Aunt Kitty gently.

'No, don't shout,' agreed Miss Gargoyle.

'Well, what about our husbands? It's been two days now and not a word!'

'What a pair of naughty boys, eh?'

'Miss Gargoyle, we know you know where they are, so please stop pretending.'

'Well, I might, and I might not. Perhaps we can come to some mutual agreement. Tit for tat, that sort of thing.'

'Really! Well, if you must,' said Aunt Winifred, crossly. 'If you want to bargain we can try and find . . . but what on earth have we got that you'd want?'

'Here's a little clue,' said Miss Gargoyle, leaning forward and winking rudely at them. 'We could make quite a game of this, couldn't we? A greenhouse. Got it? A greenhouse. Now that's not difficult, is it? But this is a special greenhouse, on a rooftop . . . a greenhouse that catches all the sun. It's got special filters and humidifiers . . . How are you getting on? Still confused? Well, now we come to the good bit. It's not the greenhouse I'm after, oh no, but a certain *flower* in that certain greenhouse . . . a certain *coloured* flower in that certain rooftop greenhouse . . . A certain *coloured* flower with spikes on the stem . . . Am I making myself clear?' she added, frowning at them. 'Beginning to get my meaning, ladies?'

Both aunts had gone pale and, for a moment, both were speechless.

'I see you do,' said Miss Gargoyle, smugly. 'Good.'

'But how did you know?' cried Aunt Kitty. 'Oh, it's just not fair. You are a cheat, Miss Gargoyle, really you are. We did you a favour giving you the job and now you repay us this way. We only employed you because you used to know Edward. And if we do know what you're talking about, and I'm not saying we do, it's nothing to do with you and you'll never have it.'

'Then you will never get your husbands back,' said Miss Gargoyle. 'It doesn't really matter much to me, either way. They're your husbands – for which you have my sympathy – and it's your problem, not mine. But if I were you, I'd think about my suggestion very seriously.'

She smiled a nasty, smug smile and then, rising with difficulty from her chair, she bowed majestically to them.

'Good evening, ladies,' she said. 'Thank you for an interesting evening, such delightful conversation . . . Until we meet again.'

Polly and Harry, not wanting to be caught spying, made a dash for it down the corridor.

'See you tomorrow!' Harry whispered as they reached the landing. 'What a to-do, eh? Didn't I tell you she had something to do with their disappearance? And, galloping gladioli, what an appetite!'

'Yes,' Polly agreed. 'She's a greedy old thing! Good gracious! I've just thought . . . you don't think she's eaten the uncles too?'

They stared at each other with horror.

Harry gulped.

'No, no, impossible! What an idea!'

'Sorry. Anyway, thanks for bringing me down to see her. I wonder what she was talking about? What did it all mean?'

Noises from below sent them scurrying apart.

'Quick! See you tomorrow. Good night!'

Polly reached the safety of her room, breathless and astounded. What had Miss Gargoyle done with Uncle Fred and Uncle Tom? What could anyone do with two grown people? And what had she meant about the greenhouse? It was very puzzling. She got undressed and into bed, sure that she wouldn't be able to sleep.

Just before she turned out the light, Morris flew in through the open window and settled

himself on the bedstead, where he listened with great interest to everything she had to tell. He clicked his beak thoughtfully, but made no comment.

The night was very quiet and still except for the distant clatter and clang in the kitchen below, where the aunts were busy clearing up, and Polly soon fell asleep.

Morris heard the distant noises and shook his head.

'Bird seed!' he muttered.

Chapter Six

As soon as breakfast was over the next morning, Polly and Harry went out into the garden together, eager for a chance to discuss the previous night's dinner party.

'Well, you must believe me now!' said Harry, triumphantly. 'She's got them somehow, somewhere, just like I said.'

'Well, she didn't *actually* say she had . . . but she was up to something, that's for sure. What was it that she wanted? I didn't understand all her clues about a greenhouse, did you?'

'No,' said Harry. 'There is a greenhouse up on Aunt Constance's roof, and I know she works away at something up there all the time, but I don't know what. Surely Miss Gargoyle wouldn't be interested in Aunt Constance's little horticultural experiments . . .?'

'Something about a special flower. Don't you

have any idea? I mean, it must be very important if Miss Gargoyle really has kidnapped your father and uncle for it.'

'Aunt Constance is just one big secret. I can't imagine what flower it could be. Actually, I hoped *you'd* know something about her experiments because it's all to do with your father.'

'My father?'

'Yes, apparently she started doing this work on her flowers and locking herself away after he left. I think they had a row. Don't you know *anything* about it?'

'No. Is that why you were surprised I'd come? It must be the reason Daddy never comes here. But I wonder why?'

'Who knows . . . maybe we'll find out more if we can find my dad.'

'What can we do?'

'I tell you what,' said Harry, 'let's have a snoop round her house. She may even have Dad and Uncle Fred hidden there!'

'But what if she catches us?'

'She won't. I heard Aunt Winifred say she had to go into town this morning, so we'll be OK if we go now. Come on, let's try it.'

'I'm not sure we should . . . but . . . OK.'

So they set off across the lawn and, taking a narrow path between some large beech trees, plunged into the depths of the garden.

'Of course, the whole place is signposted,' said Harry, as they walked along, 'but I don't need to look for directions, I know it so well. Once, years ago, Great Uncle Theopholus got lost after visiting the dovecotes and was missing for six days! He was so thin and exhausted by the time the search party found him that they didn't recognize him! That was when they decided to put in the signposts: they couldn't risk such a terrible thing happening again.'

'How dreadful!' cried Polly sympathetically. Then she caught sight of Harry's expression: his eyes were bulging and his cheeks were crimson from trying not to giggle. 'You rotten liar!' she cried. 'Oh really, Harry, I believed every word!'

Harry laughed and laughed.

'Oooh, your face!' he exclaimed. 'What a hoot! Fancy believing that rubbish!'

Polly was silent for a few moments, then she said: 'Well, naturally I believed you, because when I actually *met* Great Uncle Theopholus he was so very, very thin! And it was dreadful, you know, how just the word "dove", not to mention "dove*cotes*", drove him into a frenzy of shivers and drained every ounce of colour from his face . . . so, of course, I thought, at last, here's the reason why!'

'Pest-ridden poppies!' cried Harry. 'And I never even knew there *was* a Great Uncle Theopholus!'

'Well, there you go,' said Polly, who was looking very mischievous and trying not to laugh. 'You learn something new every day.'

'You do,' agreed Harry, frowning. 'But it's an odd coincidence, isn't it?'

Polly didn't reply.

At last they reached the lodge where Miss Gargoyle was living.

It was a small, octagonal building, which stood beside the enormous wrought-iron garden gates. These were usually locked, as visitors were not encouraged except on special days. The lodge was very pretty, with a shower of roses cascading over the yellow door. Tiny, pointed windows hung open to the fresh air, and tubs of blue pansies were arranged on the steps outside.

'Are you *sure* she's not there?' said Polly, quietly. The house looked very lived-in and suddenly she felt nervous.

'Sure,' said Harry. 'Come on, we'll just have a quick look through the windows to make

certain.'

They crept up stealthily. There were no noises
other than the birds singing and the wind rustling
in the trees.

Polly kept behind Harry as they approached
the window to look in. Not only was she scared,
but now she felt a bit ashamed: it was wrong
to spy like this. However, Polly told herself,
Miss Gargoyle had behaved so badly she didn't
deserve anything better.

The first room they looked into was the

living-room, which also doubled as a kitchen. That was empty. Then Harry went round to the back and peeped in there.

'It's the bedroom,' he told her. 'It's empty too. There are only those two main rooms, apart from the cupboards and bathroom, of course. It's very small. Come on, in we go!'

'But then your father and Uncle Fred can't be here,' said Polly cautiously.

'She might have them squeezed in under the sink,' said Harry. 'Or there may be a cellar; I wouldn't put anything past her. Oh, do come on, Polly, you can't change your mind now.'

Reluctantly, glancing nervously back over her shoulder, Polly followed Harry into the little house.

The kitchen-cum-living-room was untidy and not very clean. Old, much-used black pans were stuffed haphazardly on to bare wooden shelves and an iron kettle sat on the grate of the old-fashioned kitchen range in the wall. The fire was still warm: Miss Gargoyle hadn't been gone long. Her breakfast things were still on the table – a blue and white striped mug with big black tea leaves in it, and a soup dish made of blue tin which still held the remains of her cereal.

There wasn't anywhere there to hide two

grown men, so they went into the bedroom. Here, an ornate wooden bed covered by an orange cloth filled most of the space. Miss Gargoyle's dressing gown lay across it. Polly picked it up with interest. It was embroidered with stars, moons, flowers and strange symbols in gold thread.

'Isn't it pretty?' she said, but Harry wasn't interested.

'Let's look in here,' he said, pulling at the wardrobe door.

'Oh, Harry, you mustn't! Be careful! Don't!' But it was too late, Harry had turned the key and the doors swung open.

To Polly's relief, the wardrobe was empty except for some moth-eaten fur hats hanging on the coat hangers.

'Nothing here,' said Harry, poking his head in. Then: 'Ahh!' he cried, jumping back. 'They moved! The hats are alive!'

'What? What d'you mean?'

'They're alive! It's something furry and squeaky. Horrid!'

Keeping well back, they peered nervously into the gloomy depths of the great cupboard.

The furry, sniffling little beasts were . . . BATS!

'Oh, how horrible!' said Polly. 'Look at those skinny wings and little claws. Ugh!'

The brown bats hung in clusters from the hangers, their heads twisting and turning in the light. They twitched their noses and made little noises of surprise at being disturbed. On the floor of the wardrobe were the remains of fruit and vegetables they'd eaten. A not very pleasant smell drifted out.

'So *that's* what she wanted the fruit for!' Harry cried. 'Horrid little things. Let's close them up again. Yuk, what a thing to keep in your wardrobe!' He quickly closed and locked the doors. 'But what sort of person is she to keep things like that?' he added. 'It's so bizarre!'

'Just don't open anything else,' said Polly. 'Don't touch anything else either. In fact, why don't we go now?'

'Not yet. We might as well have a good look now we're here. Let's try the bathroom.'

'Whatever for?'

'Just to check. Come on.'

They pushed the bathroom door open gingerly and peered in.

'Looks OK,' said Harry, going in. Polly lingered in the doorway, propping the door open, as Harry went to investigate. It was an ordinary bathroom and there weren't any big cupboards. It looked OK . . . Suddenly Harry screamed. He staggered backwards, spluttering.

'What is it? Harry, what did you see?'

'Oh, golly! I don't believe it . . . Polly, go and look in the bath,' he said. 'Go on . . . it's all right, it can't get out. It just gave me a fright.'

Polly stepped cautiously towards the bath and looked down. Paddling about in a few inches of water was a baby crocodile. It looked up at her with a grin and snapped its pointed teeth with a gnash! Polly shivered.

'Phew!' she said. 'Glad it can't get out. Perhaps Miss Gargoyle's a zoologist, a secret one . . .' She stopped. Something had moved. She'd just caught sight of it from the corner of her eye. There it was, in the loo. She looked down . . . it was toads! Loads of them!

Green, brown, spotted, dappled and warty, they oozed and wobbled around the rim of the lavatory basin, their big bulging eyes blinking up at her as they gulped silently.

Polly backed out slowly. She wasn't frightened, but she didn't see any reason for getting too close.

'Toads,' she said to Harry, who hadn't come back in. 'Big ones.'

Beside the sink, she noticed three beautiful hairnets hanging from hooks on the wall. She stopped to admire them. They were fascinating constructions, delicate designs in silver thread, each with a central button or bobble. She peered at them in fascination, suddenly recognizing them.

'Look, Harry,' she said. 'Look, they're cobwebs!'

The button in the centre was in fact a spider,

and when they looked closely, they saw it was busy at work, spinning the net.

'I've seen enough,' said Harry. 'Galloping gladioli! What a house! What a woman Miss Gargoyle is!'

They went back to the relative safety of the kitchen.

'Just *what* sort of a woman, though?' said Polly. 'I mean, I've never heard of anyone keeping animals like that all over the house. Even the most enthusiastic ornithologist keeps birds out of the bathroom . . . well, usually. And cobweb hairnets? Doesn't it all begin to point towards something very spooky?'

Harry sank down on to a chair.

'What sort of spookiness? What are you thinking?' he asked. 'I'm all of a quiver. Oh, I say,' he added, glancing at the books in the shelves beside him, 'she does have some funny books: *Bat Keeping for the Amateur. One Hundred and One Hideous Hints. Things Under Stones and Other Creepy-Crawlies.*'

'I am beginning to get a very unpleasant idea,' said Polly. 'Hang on, let me have a look at those books.'

She knelt beside the bookcase and looked at the titles.

'Look!' she cried. 'Down here on the bottom shelf . . . I thought so. *Witchcraft for Beginners. Witchery Made Easy. Witch Watching* . . .' She stopped suddenly and glanced up at Harry. 'Did you hear anything?'

Harry shot out of the chair.

'Hear something? I don't need to,' he cried. 'Let's get out of here!'

Suddenly, a loud, blood-curdling squawk rang round the room and they both leaped into the air.

That was it for Harry. His face was drained of colour, his eyes staring wildly. He didn't stop to look but wrenched the door open and threw himself out into the garden. Polly was just about to follow, when the initial shock gave way to a suspicion: surely she recognized that noise . . . It was Morris.

'Pretty Polly. Pretty Polly,' sang a familiar voice, and suddenly there he was at the window.

'Oh, Morris! You naughty thing. What a fright you gave us.'

'Sorry. Couldn't resist it. You both looked so ready to be frightened somehow. Actually, I come as a warning. Miss Gargoyle's coming. Time to go. I say, I really made the cousin jump, didn't I?'

'Harry? Yes, you did.'

'Had to warn you,' said Morris. 'And they don't call me Megaphone Morris for nothing. Didn't want you to get caught. Come on.'

Harry had already plunged into the shrubs and trees surrounding the lodge and was almost invisible except for his red jumper showing between the leaves. Polly joined him just in time, for seconds later Miss Gargoyle came into view, plodding along slowly, swinging two large bags of shopping.

'That was close!' whispered Harry.

'We only made it thanks to Morris,' said Polly.

Harry looked at the bird crossly. 'There are ways of warning people and ways of warning people,' he said, 'and that wasn't one of them!'

'Well, it worked, didn't it?'

'Huh!' said Harry.

They watched Miss Gargoyle carefully, hoping they hadn't left any trace of their trespassing. She stopped at the doorway for a moment, put down her bags, and sniffed the air. She might have been admiring the scent of the roses, but there was such a horrid, suspicious look in her eyes that it was obvious she wasn't.

The two children held their breath . . .

Miss Gargoyle glanced back over her shoulder, then shrugged. Whatever she'd thought she'd smelt, now she wasn't sure. She smiled to herself, then, reaching up to the white roses, she plucked something from them and put it into her mouth. She chewed slowly, and with obvious enjoyment. Having swallowed loudly, she went into the lodge and closed the door behind her.

'Oh, oh,' moaned Harry, grabbing at his stomach and writhing. 'Did you see what she did? Oh, how awful! Dreadful!'

Polly felt quite sick.

'Disgusting,' she agreed in a weak voice.

'A caterpillar!' said Harry hoarsely. 'She ate a caterpillar – all green and wiggly, and she ate it. Oh, yuk, YUK!'

'Don't go on about it,' said Polly. 'I did see. I don't want to think about it . . . ever.'

Morris couldn't see what all the fuss was about. Although he didn't say anything, he knew from his own experience that those particular yellow-green caterpillars with the little red dots down their backs were *exceptionally* tasty!

Polly and Harry sat quietly for several minutes, trying to forget what they'd seen and to gather strength to go home.

'Well, we'd better get going,' said Harry. 'We don't want to be here when she comes out again.'

'I say, though, if she could eat a caterpillar, you don't think she could eat, er, you know, a *human* . . .'

'Polly! Don't start that again, please!'

'Sorry. Of course she wouldn't. Anyway, we didn't see any bones.'

'Polly! Crikey, that's my father you're talking about!'

'Sorry again, just teasing.'

'You're very pale. Are you all right?'

'Oh, yes, fine,' said Polly, 'it's just, well, you do realize . . .'

'What?'

'What Miss Gargoyle is.'

'I don't want to say it,' said Harry cautiously. 'I don't want it to be true. Do you think it is?'

'Yes,' said Polly. 'There's no doubt at all. Miss Gargoyle is a WITCH!'

Chapter Seven

They made their way back to The Shrubbery slowly, Morris flying on ahead and then sometimes sitting on Polly's shoulder, which Harry watched enviously.

'Interesting bird,' he said.

'He's a champion macaw.'

'He'd be a champion at sound effects. You know, things like people being strangled and tortured,' said Harry. 'If I didn't know better, I'd think he'd scared me on purpose.'

'Oh, really, Harry,' said Polly, trying not to smile. 'What a ridiculous idea!'

There was a lot to think about and much to discuss on the journey home.

'She must have put a spell on them,' said Harry. 'She must have turned them into something. Oh, just imagine, that crocodile in the bath . . . that could be my father!'

'Don't,' said Polly, remembering the toads in the loo. 'It's too terrible. Too dreadful. What are we going to do?'

'I don't know,' said Harry. 'I mean, we can't tell Mother and Aunt Winifred, they'll just think we're mad.'

'All right,' said Polly. She intended to have a good talk with Morris about it all. He was clever, he might have some good ideas. 'And then we must make a plan of some sort.'

'I have to help Mother with some seedlings after lunch,' said Harry, 'but later, at tea-time, we'll meet again. At least now we know what we're up against.'

That afternoon, after Polly had eaten a delicious lunch of fresh garden lettuce and tomatoes, cheese pie and potatoes, with plums and cream for pudding, she set out to explore the garden alone. Since it was signposted, she knew she couldn't get lost.

It was nice wandering around the lovely garden, although she wished that Morris was with her. He had disappeared to find his own lunch when they had got back to the house.

Polly knew absolutely nothing about plants, but she could identify many of the wild birds and she spotted several rare species as she strolled along. How strange that her father hadn't wanted to stay . . . he would surely have loved it here.

The first signpost she saw had three directions on it: THE MAZE, THE LILY POND and THE HOUSE. She certainly didn't want to go back to the house and the lily pond sounded interesting, so she chose that.

The path was narrow and she couldn't see much above the tall bushes so her thoughts drifted back to the awful Miss Gargoyle. She had never really believed that witches existed before today, but the evidence all pointed to it being true. Polly became so engrossed in her thoughts that she didn't notice where she was going, and suddenly she found herself surrounded by high, densely thick, privet hedge.

While she had been thinking, she had walked straight into the maze!

The path beneath her feet had changed to soft, closely clipped grass. There were no flowers. Everything was green: the tall walls were a fantastic mixture of dark green, emerald green, shiny green that was almost black, and soft yellow-greens. Polly turned round quickly and began to retrace her steps, but very soon realized that all she was doing was getting more and more hopelessly lost.

Jolly silly idea, having signposts directing you to the wrong place, she thought. How on earth am I going to get out?

After a while, she came to a bench in a clearing and sat down on it. It was hot and dusty and she was just beginning to get a little scared when, glancing up, she caught sight of a turquoise and yellow dot far above her in the sky.

Morris!

'Hey, Morris! Morris!' she yelled, waving her arms madly and trying to whistle at the same time. 'Morris! It's me. HELP!'

In no time at all, the dot materialized into Morris and he was soon beside her on the seat.

'You called, madam?' he asked, in a posh voice.

'I certainly did. Morris, I'm stuck in this beastly place.'

'You want to get out?'

'Definitely. I never wanted to get in.'

'It is signposted,' said Morris.

'Outside, Morris, but not in here. It wouldn't be very sensible to signpost a maze, would it?'

'True. True. A good point, little mistress. Don't worry, I'll soon get you out. They don't call me Maze-Puzzler Morris for nothing, you

know.' And he flew off to get an aerial view.

They don't call you Maze-Puzzler Morris at all! Polly thought, watching him soaring into the blue sky above her.

'Very easy,' Morris told her when he returned a few minutes later. 'This bench is right in the centre of the maze, and all the paths lead to it. All you have to do is keep turning to the right and you'll soon be out.'

Polly did exactly as he advised and she was soon standing in the open garden again.

'Won't you stay and explore with me, Morris,' Polly asked. 'It's boring all on my own.'

'I am your guiding light,' said the bird. 'At your command.'

The second signpost Polly saw said: THE ANCIENT RUINS, THE GREENHOUSES, and THE TOPIARY GARDEN.

'Ancient ruins sound fun,' said Polly, wistfully.

'Let's try the topiary garden,' said Morris. 'I've always fancied being immortalized in a bit of privet.'

'Oh, all right. But what is topiary?'

'You know, people have them in their front gardens: hedges cut into peacocks and horses and things. I've never seen a macaw done justice to, but no doubt that day will come. In fact, if you ever hear of anyone wanting a model . . . well, you know where to find me.'

They followed the path indicated and soon reached a clearing where the greenest, lushest grass grew that Polly had ever seen. In the centre of this emerald circle was a large pond, its surface almost hidden by plate-like lily leaves and gigantic pink and white flowers which floated on it like blobs of ice-cream.

'Oh! The lily pond!' cried Polly. 'Lovely!' And she knelt down by the water's side and dipped her hands in. It was purplish-green and thick, like shampoo. 'Isn't it glorious?' she said. 'How could Daddy have ever wanted to leave here?'

'Independence. Your mother. The birds,' said Morris in a clever voice. 'But, Polly, haven't you remembered, we *were* going to the topiary garden.'

'We must have taken the wrong path,' said Polly, reluctantly getting up. 'But it is nice here.'

'Here we are!' Morris called. 'This way!' And he flew to the next signpost.

THE HERB GARDEN, THE POTTING SHEDS and THE TOPIARY GARDEN, it said.

'Onward, oh intrepid traveller!' cried Morris, and he flew off towards the elusive topiary garden again.

They hadn't gone very far before they came to some low wooden sheds arranged in neat rows under the trees. POTTING SHEDS, said a clear notice pinned to the nearest one.

They looked inside one of the buildings: rows and rows of plant pots were carefully stacked on wooden shelves all round the walls. There was a strong smell of earth and peat and moss and summer. Polly thought it must be very nice to work there. It was sad, but true, as Polly knew from her own experience, that birds could smell dreadful if their cages weren't cleaned out regularly.

'Well,' said Morris, 'those are pots and these are sheds. What now?'

'I just don't understand it,' said Polly. 'Unless the signs are all wrong, we've made a mistake and taken the wrong path again.'

'Unless the signs are wrong,' Morris repeated. 'Why not? Suppose someone didn't want you to find the topiary garden? It would be a good way, wouldn't it?'

'But who? And why?'

'Just a whisper of a suspicion a friendly dove told me,' said Morris. 'They don't miss much. Don't be taken in by all that cooing and billing. Nothing to do with love. It's all gossip – honestly, I know . . .'

'What suspicion?'

'That Miss Gargoyle's moved them.'

'Miss Gargoyle?'

Morris flew forwards to the next signpost and beckoned for her to follow. 'Let's see,' he said, and before Polly could argue, he had disappeared down the track leading to the topiary gardens once again.

They didn't have to go far before they found themselves back at the entrance to the maze.

'See, I told you. There's some witchery about or my name's not Morris Macintosh Macaw.'

'It's not,' Polly pointed out, 'but I'm beginning to think you're right. It must be her. But why would Miss Gargoyle not want us to find the topiary garden? I must tell Harry. He should be able to find these topiary things without the signs anyway.'

'He should,' Morris agreed, 'but from what I've seen of him, he'd have trouble finding his way round a bowl of rice pudding.'

'Morris!'

'I don't like boys,' said Morris. 'Boys poke their fingers through the bars of cages. Boys shout and rush into things without thinking, and from what I've seen, Cousin Harry is *no* exception.'

Chapter Eight

After tea, Harry and Polly set out to look for the topiary garden.

'Perhaps it's moved,' Harry suggested.

'Of course!' Polly cried, in mock amazement. 'Why didn't I think of that? Topiary gardens are on the move all the time!'

'Perhaps you went down the wrong paths, then,' said Harry.

'What a brilliant idea! I mean, I can't read simple signs or anything, of course. How do you manage to be so clever?' said Polly.

'Oh, it comes naturally,' said Harry, grinning. 'I don't even have to try. Come on, it's this way.'

At the first signpost, Harry had to agree: it was pointing in the wrong direction. He swung it back to its proper position.

'D'you know,' he said, 'I think someone's

been changing these.'

'Einstein your middle name, is it? Gosh, Harry, you've so sharp you'll cut yourself one of these days!'

Harry grinned. But he did know the garden well, whatever Polly might think of him, and he did find the topiary garden without the signposts, which, Polly later thought, Morris could also have done, if he'd wanted to, by flying there.

The topiary garden was a lush green area, surrounded by very tall, clipped yew hedges. Four entrances – simply spaces in the hedge – led the way in.

The grass inside was mowed to a neat half-inch length and was greener than the greenest green paint. Walking on it was like walking on a wodge of cotton wool: it was springy and quiet beneath them.

Grass steps led down into a lower region where the darker clipped shapes and figures were arranged.

There was an extraordinary assortment of animals. There were horses rearing on long elegant legs; peacocks whose green tails fanned out in gigantic sprays of leaves and twigs; birds sitting plumply on their nests; dogs who looked as if they would bark at any moment; cats pouncing on unsuspecting mice; and fish leaping from spouts of green water, which hung suspended above the ground like green lace.

'This is all my father's work,' said Harry, proudly. 'I think he wanted to be a sculptor really.'

'They're beautiful,' said Polly. 'They don't look real but somehow they look alive.'

'They do, don't they,' Harry agreed.

'I just love them!' cried Polly and she ran amongst the figures, touching them and studying them in admiration.

Then she stopped.

She had found two life-sized green men. She stared at them. They were odd. They were definitely *very* odd.

'Harry!'

'What?'

'Harry, come here.'

'What is it?'

He strolled up to where she was standing. 'What is . . .?' he began.

Then he saw the two figures. His mouth dropped open and his eyes grew as round as marbles as he stared at them.

'Yes, they are peculiar, aren't they?' said Polly.

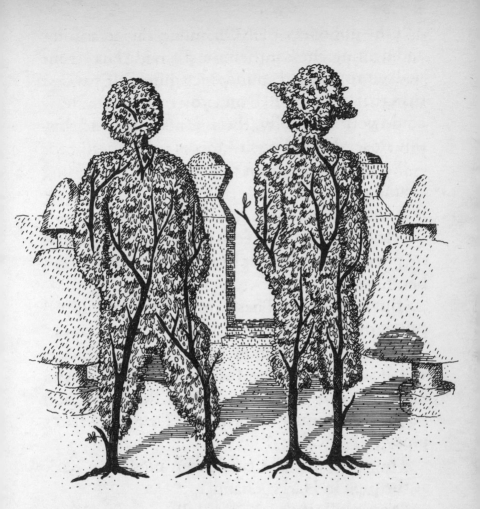

'It's not just me, is it? I mean, there's something
. . . they're all twiggy and bare, they look as
though they need a trim and anyway, they're so
ordinary! Who'd want two boring old men like
that?'

'Oh, goodness me! Oh, jumping geraniums and flaming chrysanthemums!' cried Harry as he walked round and round the figures. 'It's worse than that, far worse. Don't you realize? Oh, how could you? But Polly, this is Uncle Fred and this, this miserable old bush – this is my father!'

'What? Oh, no, don't be silly. You're teasing again!'

'I wish I were. Look, see that thing on his head? Uncle Fred's hat, he keeps his fishing hooks in it . . . in fact, see that bit of red? It's a feather on a hook.'

'But it can't be! These are just bits of clipped privet or yew. They're not people, just shapes.'

'But they're different to all the rest, thicker and heavier. And the fishing flies, Polly! And here . . .' He put his hand into the leaves and pulled out a small black pipe. 'That's my dad's pipe.'

They stared at the two green men then back at the pipe in Harry's hand.

'It's a spell, isn't it?' said Polly.

'It must be!' said Harry. 'Oh, that rotten Miss Gargoyle! Much better than hiding them in her house, of course, since nobody ever comes here except my father really. Better even than turning them into toads or bats. But she's been *too* clever!

We wouldn't have even looked here if she hadn't changed the signposts!'

He stared miserably at the two figures.

'Let's tell the grown-ups,' said Polly. 'Don't you think they would believe she's a witch if they saw these two? They would think of something.'

'No! No, we can't! Mother would simply die if she saw Dad like this!'

'So? What do you suggest?'

'Leave things to me. I'll think of something.'

'Like what?' asked Polly crossly. 'And why should I leave it to you? You don't plan anything, you just *do* things without thinking. You're bound to make a mess of it.'

'Well, it's my father and I'll make a mess if I want to!'

'Typical,' said Polly. 'Totally unreasonable.'

'I've a right to be,' said Harry. 'Just look at my poor dad!'

'I know,' said Polly, more gently, 'it is awful, but surely I can help. Surely your mother could help.'

'Well, later, perhaps, but don't tell her yet. Promise!'

'I promise,' said Polly, glumly.

Boys! she thought. Everything Morris says

about them is true! She couldn't trust Harry not to do something silly.

'Come on,' said Harry. 'Let's go. I can't bear to see Dad like that.'

They trudged gloomily back to the house. Harry was very quiet, and Polly guessed that he was finding the shock hard to take.

'The house is just over there,' he said suddenly, pointing over some bushes to where the roof was visible. 'You go on ahead, Polly, I think I'll just go on and see how the pelargonium cuttings are coming along.'

'Are you sure? You won't do anything daft, will you?'

'No. I just . . . I'll see you later.' And he slouched off along another path, head down and shoulders drooping.

Polly carried on alone.

'Silly boy,' she said out loud. 'Stupid numb-skulled nit. We need a plan. We need to think. Why won't he THINK?'

There was a sudden whirring in the air above her head and a voice said: 'Evening, Polly.'

'Oh, Morris!'

'The one and only!' agreed Morris, swirling down to join her. He rested on her shoulder and pecked fondly at her neck. 'You really must

remember to wash behind your ears, Polly dear,'
he said.

'I've got far more important things to think
about just now,' she said shortly.

'To whom were you referring?' said Morris.
'Who won't think?'

'My cousin,' said Polly.

'Oh, that specimen of boyhood. You need a
brain to think.'

'He has got a brain . . . well, a small one,'
said Polly, laughing. 'It was very naughty of you
to scare him like that this morning,' she added.
'You very nearly scared me too.'

Morris tweaked her ear apologetically.

'So what's he done now?'

'He won't let me tell the aunts what we've
found. We've been to the topiary garden,' said
Polly. 'We've discovered my uncles.'

'So that's where they were! I thought they
might be.'

'Did you?'

'Well, news does fly fast up there in the air.
There were one or two suggestions . . .'

'They've been turned into bushes,' said Polly.
'Topiary bushes in the topiary garden! Isn't it
dreadful?'

'I shouldn't think they mind much. They're

great gardeners themselves, after all.'

'Oh, Morris! But it's terrible and Harry won't let me do anything! What shall we do?'

'Let's just wait a while,' said Morris. 'It takes time to develop a really well-laid plan of attack. Uh, oh, there's an aunt – it's the one with feathers in her hat too, and since I'm very partial to mine, I'm off. See you later.' He soared into the air and disappeared, just as Aunt Winifred arrived.

'There you are! At last! Aunt Constance wants to see you.'

Aunt Constance? There had been so much going on that Polly had forgotten all about her Aunt Constance, the aunt who rarely came downstairs, but lived all the time in her room, working on secret plants in her greenhouse.

'Coming,' said Polly and, putting the strange leafy figures to the back of her mind, she followed Aunt Winifred towards the house.

Chapter Nine

'Do hurry, Polly,' Aunt Winifred muttered.
'Where have you been? Has that naughty Harry
been looking after you? Come along, Constance
is waiting. It's bad to keep her waiting, she gets
very agitated and that just makes her worse.'

'Worse than what?' Polly asked.

'Worse than ever.'

'Is she ill?'

'Not really,' said Aunt Winifred. She sighed.
'Come on, follow me.'

Aunt Winifred led Polly up the main staircase
and then they branched off along a corridor to a
small spiral staircase which wound upwards, right
to the very top of the house. When they were
almost to the top, Aunt Winifred continued: 'She
set her heart on the project – oh, many years ago –
and it's become a passion now. She can't rest, she
can't think about anything else except . . .'

'Except?'

'Shh, here we are.'

They had stopped outside a narrow blue door. A brass plate on it said: PRIVATE.

Aunt Winifred took a deep breath and knocked. A voice from inside told them to come in, and Aunt Winifred opened the door, pushed Polly gently inside and closed it behind her.

Polly found herself in a large, bright room; it was a combination of bedroom, office and sitting-room. A giant-sized four-poster bed draped with blue curtains stood against one wall; there was a large wardrobe, several dark chests of drawers, two armchairs and a blue and white striped sofa. A wide, busy-looking desk occupied another wall. The carpet was blue and the wallpaper had blue butterflies dancing around blue flowers. Some of the furniture, Polly noticed, had the same hand-painted bees and flowers on it as in her own room.

Seated in one of the smaller chairs was Aunt Constance. She was older than the other aunts and was tall and thin, like a stick. The frail hand, poised elegantly on the arm of the chair, was like a twisted branch.

'So you are Edward's child?'

'Yes, Aunt Constance.'

'You don't look like him. Has he told you all about us? Does he tell you terrible lies about us all?'

'No, no he doesn't! He would never do that! Actually, I'm afraid, I hardly knew anything about you until I came.'

'Your father would like to forget us all no doubt. That's a guilty conscience for you! Come here.'

She got up slowly and went across to the french windows which she opened, then beckoned Polly to follow.

Polly saw that the doors led out on to a wide, flat, roof terrace, in the centre of which was a greenhouse.

This must be the greenhouse Miss Gargoyle mentioned, Polly thought, and she wondered if she was going to be allowed to look inside. Would she see this mysterious plant the witch seemed so interested in?

'I have hardly left these rooms since your father went,' said Aunt Constance. 'Your father took away something very precious to me.'

'Have you asked for it back?' said Polly, who couldn't believe her father would ever steal.

'Don't be silly, child. He took himself away and his brains away, he couldn't have left those, and yet . . . Does he have a greenhouse?'

'Yes.'

'He does?' She was suddenly alert and, grabbing hold of Polly's arm, she hissed: 'And what's in it, that's what I'd like to know? What does he grow?'

'Oh,' said Polly, nervously, 'you know, geraniums, cucumbers, that sort of thing.'

'Pah!' said Aunt Constance. 'You wouldn't

know a geranium from a prize dahlia, would you?'

'No,' said Polly. 'But I know a lesser spotted yellow warbler when I see one.'

'What use is that?'

'Well, it means I know it's not a *greater* spotted yellow warbler,' said Polly, 'and that might be important, specially to another lesser spotted yellow warbler.'

'So, you know nothing about plants.'

'No.'

'Then you won't be much use to us . . . I don't suppose you'd even want to see what I'm growing here, then?' She pointed to the greenhouse.

'Oh, but yes, please,' said Polly.

'Well, you can't.' She stared down at Polly but although she sounded cross, Polly could see that she wasn't really. Her expression was more sad than anything else. 'It's private. It's all private and secret. Why did he leave us, do you think?' she asked more gently.

'Oh, independence. Mother. The birds,' said Polly, vaguely remembering what Morris had said. 'But I don't really know. *I* wouldn't have ever left. I think it's lovely!'

'We never wanted him to leave us. We were

jealous, I suppose, that he wanted to branch out, that he'd had enough of the flowers and wanted Margaret . . . Tell him we're still trying,' said Aunt Constance. 'Tell him,' and she lowered her voice to a whisper, 'tell him, we're nearly there.'

'I will,' Polly promised, more puzzled than ever.

'Very well, you can go now . . . and Polly?'

'Yes, Aunt Constance?'

'Go and look at the roses. Go and smell them. Go and touch them. Go and look at their colours.

You must understand why there is no flower more perfect than a rose.'

'Yes, Aunt Constance.'

'Goodbye then.'

Aunt Constance took a key from her pocket, opened the door to the greenhouse and locked herself inside it. Polly stared for a few moments at her aunt, now surrounded by greenery, then tiptoed back through the french windows, back through the blue room and down to her own little bedroom in the round tower.

She still had no idea what her aunt had meant by her strange conversation, or why she had been called to her room.

Chapter Ten

The following morning the sun was streaming in through the window and Morris was already preening himself on the end of Polly's bed when she woke up.

'Good morning!' he said. 'Sleep well, oh my princess of the night?'

'No,' said Polly, irritably. 'I had awful dreams; they've all got me so confused. What did Daddy take and why won't he give it back and why won't anybody just say things straight out instead of all this round-about mysteriousness?'

'Because they are grown-ups, Polly my dear. Stick to birds and children . . . well, *some* children, that's my advice.'

When Polly was dressed she checked the plant her father had given her. The flower buds were just about to open. Soon she would be able to give it to her aunts.

'It just looks like a rose to me,' she said to Morris. 'But after talking to Aunt Constance, it may turn out to be a pansy – I don't know. I'll give it a drop of water, it's a bit dry.'

'Any plans for un-hedging the uncles?' asked Morris.

'Not yet. I'll give Harry one more chance and then we'll leap into action. OK?'

'If you think he deserves . . .' Morris began.

But Polly interrupted him with a cry of surprise. She had just caught sight of something moving in the garden below.

'Look down there!' she cried, pointing to the garden. 'Look, there's Harry. Can you see? Why is he creeping about behind the bushes and looking so sneaky? Oh, Morris, don't you just bet he's going off to see Miss Gargoyle without me?'

'I'm rather afraid I do.'

'Morris, we can't let him get away with this. You fly down and follow him. Don't let him out of your sight and I'll be down as quickly as I can.'

'Certainly. No problem. Why, in the detective world I'm known as Morris the Marvellous Magic-Eye.' And, with a wink, he launched himself off the balcony and swooped away over the treetops.

Meanwhile, Polly hurried downstairs as fast as she could and set off in pursuit.

As she had guessed, by the time it took her to reach the garden, Harry had disappeared. She set off in the direction she'd last spotted him and, minutes later, glimpsed Morris far above her in the sky. Using him as a guide, she followed.

She seemed to have been walking for a very long time before at last Morris flew down to join her.

'Well, I know where he is,' he said. 'And you're not going to like it. It's witchery again.'

'He's gone to the lodge?'

'Yes. It's just round the next corner, over there by the big cypress tree.'

'I'd never have recognized it,' said Polly, looking round. 'But of course he'd come here! Silly nit!'

The little lodge looked the same as the day before, except this time smoke streamed out of the chimney and Miss Gargoyle's washing was hanging on the line. There was something so fantastic about her enormous woolly red bloomers flapping like sails in the morning breeze, that this time Polly couldn't feel nervous.

'I wonder if she knows we know about the

topiary figures,' she said.

'I shouldn't think so.'

'Golly, I hope Harry hasn't gone in. Do you think he has?'

'He was here a moment ago,' said Morris. 'He's either inside or been sensible and gone home . . . not much chance of that, I suppose!'

'We'd better go and see. I hope we aren't too late, she might change him into a frog or something.'

'It wouldn't much matter if she did,' said Morris, his beady eyes shining mischievously, 'nobody would notice the difference!'

They crept forward and peeped in through the open kitchen window.

The table was laid for breakfast and a fire burnt in the grate. Miss Gargoyle, a grim, unfriendly expression on her round face, was sitting at the table. Her black eyes, shining like marinated olives, watched Harry intently.

Harry was standing by the range with his hands on his hips. Two bright red patches burned in his cheeks – not because he was too close to the fire, but because he was cross and worried. His voice sounded strained and loud.

'. . . It's no good denying it, no good at all,' he was saying. 'You're a witch and you've put a

spell on my father. You're a witch and I've got proof you're a witch and I'm going to go to the police.'

Miss Gargoyle smiled at him, a humourless smile which didn't do more than crinkle her thin upper lip. She patted her hair complacently, poking her plaits into place and stroking a long curl over her shoulder.

'The police, eh? What on earth for? What would they care about a silly little boy and his wild stories. Really, Hairy . . .'

'My name's Harry!'

'Hairy. Harry. What's the difference? So, anyway my little friend, what is this proof you've got?'

'I've seen them!' Harry cried, triumphantly. 'I've been to the topiary garden and seen them both. You can't say they're not there. You can't!'

'You've seen them, have you? Well, well. And how are they? No greenfly, I hope. I've been *most* worried about mildew.'

'Don't joke about it,' said Harry crossly. 'It was a terrible thing to do.'

'Terrible,' agreed Miss Gargoyle, mildly. 'Really, Hairy, I haven't the slightest idea what you're talking about. Do you mean you think those green men I spent so long clipping into shape have something to do with your father and uncle? Is that it?'

'Yes,' said Harry, beginning to get worried. 'Aren't they?'

'Well, of course they are – in a way, since they're *copies* of your dear relations, but that's all. What else could they possibly be?'

'But, but . . .' Harry began to feel very unsure. 'They're different from the rest. Not as nice. They *are* your spells, I'm sure they are . . . aren't they?' he asked. 'Aren't they magic?'

'Oh, dear, all this witch nonsense,' said Miss Gargoyle. 'I really don't know where you get such ideas. Now, calm down, my lamb,' she added sweetly, 'and have a nice cup of tea, won't you? I haven't had my breakfast yet and I can't do a thing without my morning cuppa.' Her eyes twinkled suddenly and she smiled fondly at him. 'A nice cup of tea?' she repeated.

'Thank you. Yes,' said Harry, as if in a daze.

'Sugar?'

'Three, please,' said Harry, sinking down in the rocking chair. His gaze fell on the books beside him and suddenly he was alert again. 'But, hang on,' he said, 'what about these? Nobody ordinary has books like this: *Bat Keeping for the Amateur, Witches and Their Ways* . . .'

'Who said I was ordinary?' mumbled Miss Gargoyle. 'Anyway, I'm interested in lots of things.'

'So I see,' said Harry. 'It makes me think you could be dangerous, knowing all this stuff.'

Miss Gargoyle burst into laughter: it sounded like someone choking at the bottom of a cavernous drain.

'What a comic you are!' she spluttered. 'Me dangerous! All I've done is show off my horticultural expertise, that's all. Shown my appreciation of the male form. And don't take any notice of those books there. They're Mother's.'

Suddenly Harry leapt out of the chair again as yet another thought struck him.

'And the bats!' he cried. 'The crocodile!'

Miss Gargoyle's face grew suddenly hard and sharp. The rosy colour faded from her apple-like cheeks, turning them to grey. Then a sickly green colour diffused her face.

'Bats?' she said in a choked voice. 'Crocodile? Now what on earth are you talking about?' There was a bleak, unfriendly expression in her eyes.

Harry blushed. He trembled as he realized his mistake – now it was obvious he'd been spying.

'I mean, I mean,' he stammered, 'I peeped through the window and saw them. Things in the bathroom . . .'

Suddenly Miss Gargoyle was charming and reassuring again.

'Mother's,' she said lightly. 'She's been staying. She's keen on reptiles . . . must be why she married my dad!' she giggled. 'Seriously, she studies them. Bats too. Everything. She's a rum one, is my mum.' She flashed another wide smile at poor confused Harry. 'Happy now?' she asked, turning her back to make the tea.

Harry put his head in his hands and moaned.

He was all in a muddle. He couldn't think straight. He'd forgotten what he'd come for. He'd forgotten what he was supposed to be saying. Why hadn't he made a proper plan?

Miss Gargoyle busied herself making the tea.

She was most careful to keep her back to him. Snatching a quick glance over her shoulder to

check he wasn't looking, she took a little brown book furtively from one of the numerous pockets of her voluminous overalls. Harry couldn't see it or what was written on the cover, but Polly and Morris could see. It said . . . SPELLS! Quickly she leafed through its pages. When she'd found the right place, she took down a big green tin from a high shelf. The very large, clear letters on its side said: EXTRA-SUPER HEDGE FERTILIZER.

'You did say three?' she asked, spooning three heaped spoonfuls of the tin's purple crystals into his cup. 'Didn't you?'

She stirred the fertilizer rapidly into his drink, and all the while read silently from her little book.

'There!' said Miss Gargoyle, spinning round. 'Chin, chin.' And she handed him the cup.

'Thanks. Oh, this is nice,' said Harry, smacking his lips. 'What an unusual flavour. Is it one of those herbal teas?'

'Yes,' said Miss Gargoyle. 'Hedge flavour.' And she began to chortle.

'Pardon?'

'I said *hedge flavour*. If you'd just care to look down at your feet,' she said, 'you'll know what I mean.'

Bewildered, Harry did as she suggested.

His feet weren't there.

Where they should have been were now two stumpy trunks from which sprouted privet leaves. His hands and arms too, now he looked at them, were covered in leaves and more were sprouting out every second. He opened his mouth to speak, but no words came.

Privet hedges cannot speak.

It took only a few moments for the transformation to take place and then all that remained was a twiggy green figure of a boy which bore very little resemblance to the original Harry at all.

'There now, you silly boy,' said Miss Gargoyle in a kindly voice. 'Painless, wasn't it? All over now. I'll put you out with the others. Just a touch of this,' she added, spraying him from a garden spray, 'to keep the leaves green and the aphids away, and you're all done!' She giggled again. 'Silly boy.' Then she picked him up and, whistling softly, carried him out into the garden and disappeared with him amongst the trees.

Polly stared at Morris. She was speechless, and even Morris, for a few seconds, could think of nothing to say. At last, he clicked his beak, shaking his head.

'Well, well,' he muttered, 'better than a toad, I suppose.'

'Poor Harry!' cried Polly. 'I wanted to stop it. To do something, but I just couldn't!'

'There wasn't anything we could do,' said Morris, calmly. 'Look on the bright side, at least he's with his father now.'

'And why did he believe her? He forgot about the caterpillar. He must have completely forgotten about the things she said at the dinner party too. What a nit!'

'What a nit, as you so succinctly put it,' Morris agreed, preening his feathers. 'Now . . . I think . . . while she's gone . . . Come on, Polly, let's just sneak a quick look. I'm pretty sure she left her spell book on the table when she went. We could take it before she gets back.'

'Dare we?'

''Course we dare. Go on, in you go.'

Everything was quiet. It would take Miss Gargoyle several minutes to reach the topiary garden and plant poor Harry there. So Polly took a big breath and marched into the lodge.

Beneath the shelves where the magic potion had been was a small brown book. Polly opened it. On the flyleaf inside, it said:

This book belongs to:

Gertie Gargoyle

~~Bogweed Cottage~~ The Lodge
~~Bogweed Park~~ The Shrubbery
Dorset
England
Europe
The World
The Universe
Space

'Proof!' cried Polly. 'Not that I needed any more, but the aunts'll have to believe this!'

'Come on then, Polly, let's get going. Breakfast was ages ago and I'm hungry.'

'But do look at this writing,' said Polly, as she flicked through the pages of the book. 'It's weird!'

The pages were covered with a strange, magic writing, all squiggles, dots and dashes. In some places there were real words, as if, occasionally, the magic writing had proved too difficult and someone had written in the meaning. Page twenty-one had been much used; it had many pencil marks and was smeared with what appeared to be plum jam. Written in large letters at the top of the page were the words: TOPIARY and PRIVET.

'This must be it!' Polly said. 'I do wish we could read it, we might be able to undo it . . . Gosh, why are we hanging about? Come on, Morris, let's get out of here!'

She tucked the spell book into the top of her trousers and they hurried outside again.

There was no point in trying to find Harry, he would already be with his father and uncle in the topiary garden, so they set off towards The Shrubbery instead. And this time, Polly thought, she *would* tell her aunts.

Polly walked quickly, Morris flying beside her, and they soon came to a path they thought they recognized.

'Nearly there,' Polly said. 'I think we're close to the maze. It will be such a relief to tell the aunts everything!'

But then, suddenly, just as she rounded a great oak tree, she was forced to a halt. There, right in front of her, was Miss Gargoyle herself!

Chapter Eleven

'Oh!' they both exclaimed.

'You!' cried Polly.

'Me?' said Miss Gargoyle. 'Well, of course I'm me! Who,' she said, drawing herself up to her full height, 'are you?'

'Polly.'

'Polly? Polly who?'

Then she saw the spell book.

'Oh, toads and warts! What's that?' she cried, pointing her long, podgy finger accusingly at the brown book.

'Glancing down, Polly saw the spell book jutting out of her trouser top. Why hadn't she hidden it? Quickly she put her hand over it and stepped backwards.

'Nothing,' she said.

'Nothing?' cried Miss Gargoyle. 'NOTH-ING? That's my spell book!' she screeched, lunging out at it. But Polly was too quick and darted out of the way.

'Rats' ears and bats' bums!' shrieked the witch. 'Come back here!' She charged down the path after Polly like an angry bull. 'You won't get away!' she yelled as she chased Polly. 'Come back! Come back!'

Polly ran for all she was worth. She had come second in the school 100 metres race earlier that year; if Miss Gargoyle had been chasing her then, she would have come first.

The witch was quite fast too, despite her size, but she wasn't as nimble as Polly. Even so, as she ran, Polly thought that at any moment she would feel the witch's hand on her back or her feet catch on her heels.

'Morris! Morris!' Polly cried as she hurtled along. 'What shall I do? MORRIS! Help! What shall I do?'

Morris was darting around in front of her, urging her on.

'The maze, Polly. It's just over there. It's your only chance,' he called back. 'Try and lose her in there. I bet she doesn't know the way out and we've got her book: she can't turn you into anything without that!'

Breathing heavily, her heart pounding painfully against her ribs, Polly dived into the comforting green corridors of the maze.

Immediately she felt better. The soft grassy paths absorbed the noise of her footsteps and the surrounding green walls were reassuring and quickly hid her from view. Rabbit-like she zigzagged her way into its depths, hoping as she did so that Miss Gargoyle had been left far behind.

When she was too out of breath to go any further she stopped and, sinking down on to the mossy floor, inhaled deeply and listened.

She strained her ears: somewhere near and drawing closer all the time, was Miss Gargoyle. She could hear her hoarse breathing and the soft rustle as she brushed against the bushes. Polly held her breath. The witch was close, so close . . . closer . . . She was there! Just inches away on the other side of the privet wall!

It was lucky that the witch chose the paths she did: if she had turned a different corner, taken a left-hand path instead of a right-hand one, or a right instead of a left, she might have caught Polly, but she didn't and by the time she stopped she had had enough. She sat down where she was and, after a few seconds, she began to speak.

'Poggy? Poggy?' she called. 'Where are you?

You little worm,' she added under her breath. 'I know you're not far away.'

Polly didn't move. Her heart beat so loudly she was sure Miss Gargoyle would hear it.

'Poggy, my dear, don't be obstinate. Why, I know you're there, I can *smell* you!'

Polly remembered how Miss Gargoyle had sniffed outside the lodge after she and Harry had been there. She must have been smelling them!

'My name's Polly!' Polly said. She couldn't bear being so close to the witch, and slowly got up and took a couple of steps away from the hedge. 'And yes, I will be obstinate,' she added.

There was an increase in the rustling noise from the other side and, as Polly moved away, she saw something stirring amongst the leaves. Polly stared. For a few moments she thought it was an animal of some sort, then, with a gulp of alarm, she recognized it; it was the witch's hand!

Her long fat fingers were creeping through the twiggy parts of the bottom of the hedge, as if they had a life of their own and weren't attached to any body at all, and all the time the witch went on talking.

'Poggy suits you better,' she said slyly, 'at least

it will when I've turned you into a slime-smelly little toad. Hee, hee.'

Miss Gargoyle's hand crept further and further through the leaves. It was like a large pale spider, inching closer to Polly every second.

'You'll find that a trifle difficult without the spell book,' said Polly, trying to sound calm. She crept backwards, all the time keeping her eyes fixed on the moving hand. Suddenly she bumped into something. Glancing round she saw it was a large upturned plant pot. Quickly she stepped up on it: she felt safer off the ground.

Still Miss Gargoyle's hand approached, her arm growing longer and longer. Like a pale writhing snake it stretched across the path until her fingers were touching the plant pot. They felt all round the rim, walked round it one way and then the other, then they began to climb up it.

It was too much. Polly screamed. Almost at the same moment, just seconds before the long, elastic arm reached her, Morris jumped down and pecked it. Hard!

'Yeow!' cried Miss Gargoyle, and her arm recoiled like a worm hit by a spade and slid back under the hedge.

There followed a couple of moments' silence while the two parties drew breath.

Then the witch began again.

'I don't actually have my brown spell book, that's true, dearie,' agreed the witch sweetly, 'but there are other things I can do, as you've just seen. By the way, you've got very sharp nails for such a wee girl. Yes, there are other things I can do. I mean, you don't need a spell to snip a few branches off an old hedge, do you?

Or a bit of weedkiller in a big spray gun? Now, that might be *very* unpleasant for some certain topiary bushes I could mention. Hand over my book, Miss Clever Cloggs, or else!'

'Never,' said Polly, clasping the book even tighter. 'Never!'

'Little stinker!' said Miss Gargoyle. 'All right. All right. Keep it. I didn't want to cheat. I didn't want all this trouble but you asked for it. Keep the book, and much good may it do you. You'll never be able to read the spells and I shan't help . . .' She paused. 'Don't you think, couldn't you consider, that perhaps we could come to some agreement?'

'No, I do not!' said Polly, trying to express a confidence she did not feel.

'Then you force me to take action.'

'You already have.'

'Different action. Meaner action.'

Polly lowered her voice to a whisper. 'But, Morris, what *are* we going to do?'

'I've got an idea,' he whispered back. 'It's not for nothing I'm known as Mischief-Maker Morris, you know. It won't stop her, only delay her. We just need enough time for you to get the book to the aunts and get their help. Off you go, and run like the wind.'

121

Polly didn't wait to hear more. She nodded her agreement and very quietly crept out of the maze and hurried towards the house.

'Poggy! Poggy!' cried Miss Gargoyle. 'What are you up to? Where are you going?' She began to heave herself up to her feet. 'I'm coming after you!'

Quickly, Morris pushed his way between the leaves of the hedge and, remembering the inscription in the spell book, he began to call in a high-pitched, sing-song voice.

'Gertie! Oh, Gertie!' he trilled.

Miss Gargoyle stopped and spun round.

There was no one there!

Her eyes narrowed and she frowned. Who was calling and where were they?

'Gertie, yoo hoo, Gertie,' the strange little voice sang.

'Hello,' she ventured at last.

'Hello, Gertie,' said the voice more sternly. 'Can you see me?'

'No . . . where are you?'

'Here, right in front of you. I'm not hiding. If you can't see me it's because you've got no insight. That's what being bad does, Gertie, and you've been *very* bad.'

'Oh, tosh!' said the witch rudely. But she

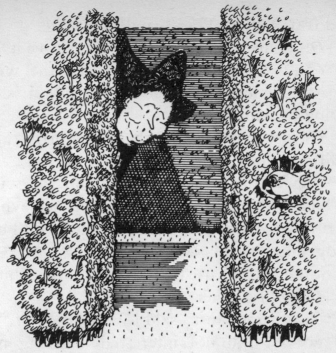

couldn't resist having a good look. She tiptoed across the path and peered behind the hedges, she looked round each corner and into the deepest shadows, she even lifted a few large stones before giving up at last and sitting down again.

'Absolute baloney,' she said. 'There's no one there.'

'Gertie,' Morris went on, 'I see a dark shadow over your head; a cloud of darkness and trouble.'

'What drivel,' said Miss Gargoyle, glancing up quickly and seeing nothing. 'Compost heaps and rotten eggs. There's nothing there.'

'Yes there is, Gertie, but you can't see it.'

'You're wasting my time,' said the witch, crossly, which was precisely what Morris was trying to achieve.

'You are a very bad witch,' said Morris, trying a different tack. 'Your spells are evil and . . .'

'They're not exactly good,' said the witch. 'Which witch's spells are? If you see what I mean. Mine are OK, give or take the odd dead hedgehog.'

'Some witches use their magic for nice things, for delighting others and . . .'

'Oh, give it a rest,' said Miss Gargoyle. 'You do go on. I'm not interested in being nice. Nobody is nice to me. I'm a horrid witch and that's all there is to it. Mind you,' she added, 'it's not quite the vocation I'd planned for myself.' She sat down and leaned back against the hedge wall, folding her arms: she had quite forgotten whom she was talking to and why. 'I'm very good with potting compost and fertilizers, no one can deny that – and I'm a fair cook – but what I did always want, was to be a shorthand typist . . .'

'Good Lord!' squeaked Morris.

'It's true, though,' said Miss Gargoyle. 'Only

Mum said my hands weren't short enough and it was so very hard to learn. Then I thought about being a hairdresser – I've got such lovely hair of my own, you see – and then I met Edward.'

'Edward?'

'Edward, he's their brother, you know. At the horticulture college it was. He never said it, but I knew he loved me. He was working on a rose. Oh, what a rose! I could have helped. Together we could have done it, but no, that mouse-featured Margaret had to come and steal him away. It was a long time ago . . . but I felt . . . I knew it was complete. The rose was here . . .

'I'm not really anything now, though as Mum says, and she's smart, you don't choose witchery, it chooses you, so I suppose I'll always be a witch. Now . . .' she had closed her eyes and was breathing slowly and calmly, 'go away, will you. I have things to think about.'

Morris climbed quietly out of his hiding place in the privet wall, but the rustling noises disturbed the witch and she shot upright again, frowning.

'What's up? What's been going on? Where's that voice? Where's that Poggy gone?'

Morris didn't answer. His little game had

worked quite well and he had learnt a lot about the witch, but he couldn't hope to detain her any longer, so he flew quietly away.

It only took Miss Gargoyle a few minutes to realize that somehow she had been tricked. With a cry of dismay, she leapt up, looking angrily around her.

'How do you get out of here?' she cried. 'Stupid hedges! Stupid puzzle!' She scrambled up and tottered off, turning first left and then right and then spinning round and going back the way she had come.

I must get to the statues, she thought. My three green men! Oh dear, if only I could remember how to make my neck long I could look over these silly walls! Hurry, hurry, she urged herself. Oh, for my spell book! Oh, what I wouldn't do for my rake! Got to get there first! Got to get to the topiary garden, quickly. QUICK!

As soon as Polly got out of the maze she ran to the house, where she found Aunt Winifred and Aunt Kitty having coffee in the kitchen.

'Hello, Polly, dear,' said Aunt Kitty. 'Have you had your breakfast already? I didn't see you earlier. Gosh, you do look hot? Been running? I don't suppose you know where that bad boy

Harry is, do you?'

'Yes, yes I do,' panted Polly. 'Oh, gosh, Aunt Kitty, it's dreadful.' And, keeping as calm as she could, she told them both what had happened and where the missing members of the family were.

At first her story was met with a stony silence, and then Aunt Winifred said: 'Polly, you can't possibly expect us to believe this.'

'Why not?' Polly asked. 'I mean, I don't want to sound rude, but why on earth would I make such a story up?'

'Well, that's true enough,' said Aunt Kitty. 'Why would she?'

'And we've certainly always thought Miss Gargoyle a little strange. Odd hairstyles, of course . . . Where is this book of spells then?' asked Aunt Winifred.

Polly handed it to her.

'This is it. See, it's all in magic writing.'

'Doesn't look very magic to me,' said Aunt Winifred. 'In fact, it reminds me of something . . . now, what on earth . . .? Perhaps Constance would know, she's very good on foreign languages and that sort of thing. Are you sure this is the book she used?'

'Yes.' Polly showed them Miss Gargoyle's

name on the flyleaf. 'It's even got SPELLS written on it! You must believe me. And, please, we must hurry,' urged Polly. 'They're in danger! Miss Gargoyle is stuck in the maze now, but not for long! As soon as she gets out – well, she could do anything to those bushes!'

'I see, yes. Immediate action. Right. Polly, go upstairs and tell Aunt Constance everything. She is wonderful in a crisis. She's also clever. We'll go to the topiary garden now . . . and keep guard.'

'Oh dear, it's miles away,' said Aunt Kitty. 'It'll take ages!'

'We'll go on the tandem!'

'Tandem?' shrieked Aunt Kitty in dismay.

'Well, can you think of anything better?' said Aunt Winifred.

'No,' Aunt Kitty agreed, 'but I haven't ridden since I was a student. Oh, dear!'

'I haven't ridden for fifteen years,' said Aunt Winifred, 'but we've no time to worry about that. Come on!'

Polly dashed upstairs and knocked loudly on Aunt Constance's door. There was no response. She knocked again and listened but when there was still no sign of her aunt, she opened the door

gingerly and went in.

The room was empty, but the french windows

were open so Polly went out on to the roof terrace.

Aunt Constance was in the depths of the greenhouse, almost completely hidden by the surrounding plants. She was crooning and murmuring to them, caressing their petals and leaves as she did so. It seemed to Polly that, in return, the plants too were reaching out to her with their leaves, eager for her touch.

She knocked timidly on the glass door.

'Hello,' she said softly. 'Hello, Aunt Constance. It's me, Polly.'

Aunt Constance spun round as if she'd been stung.

'Polly! What are you doing here? Who told you to come in?'

'Nobody. Sorry, it's an emergency. We've found Uncle Fred and Uncle Tom!'

'Were they missing? Oh, yes, I remember something about them going to a seed conference . . . waste of time in my opinion. And you've found them? Well done, where are they?' She looked past Polly's shoulder as if expecting them to appear.

'Well, we've found them but they're not here. It seems Miss Gargoyle is a witch and I'm afraid she turned them into privet hedges. Now she's turned poor Harry into one too. They're in the topiary garden and she's going to kill them with weedkiller. We've got to go and stop her.'

Instead of screaming or stamping her feet, or fainting, as Polly thought she might, Aunt Constance pressed her lips into a grim smile.

'Well, of course,' she said. 'Why not? A witch, eh? Wicked woman. Of course, she's known about this all the time.'

'Known about what?' asked Polly.

'Why, this. Our rose. This is what she's been after all along.'

Aunt Constance stood back to reveal the precious flowers she had been talking to. There were several different varieties, but the plants in the centre were roses and it was to these that she pointed.

'See this? This little beauty is our blue rose. The only one of its kind in the whole world.'

Polly peered at the small, rather dull grey rose. 'It's not very blue,' she said quietly.

'It's the bluest rose any gardener has ever made,' snapped Aunt Constance. 'And Miss Gargoyle wants it. Kitty told me something about how she wanted it . . . I didn't really take it in.'

'Now I remember,' said Polly excitedly. 'She

talked about a special flower at that dinner, but I didn't understand! And this is it! Is it really the only one in the whole world? You're not going to give it to her! You can't! You've grown it. It's yours.'

'It wasn't part of my plans, of course, but now . . . Well, how else are we going to get Fred and Tom back?'

'Well, I don't know,' said Polly. 'But we'll think of something! But later. Come on, we've got to get to the topiary garden!'

Chapter Twelve

From all corners of the grounds, people were converging on the topiary garden. At least, that was everyone's intention. Miss Gargoyle had taken a long time to find her way through the intricate corridors of the maze, and now that she had, she was walking in the *wrong* direction.

The reason she was walking in the wrong direction was that she had quite forgotten the signposts.

Miss Gargoyle had spent a long time altering them to send people off to the far corners of the garden rather than let them come across the topiary figures, but she had forgotten that, and now *she* was following them . . . and was heading towards the marble fountain. She was so busy planning horrible things to do when she reached the topiary garden that she never spared a thought to her surroundings and didn't do more than glance up now and again to check which turning to take, otherwise she might have remembered.

The witch was not progressing very quickly. The magic she had used to lengthen her arm hadn't been absolutely successful – in fact, that arm was still longer than the other – and the effort had exhausted her. She really did need her spell book, whatever she might have said.

Somewhere along the way, she had collected an enormous pair of hedge clippers and every now and then she stopped to swing them round above her head, as if she were practising for the Olympic Games. She also had to rest to draw breath as with each step she let out a stream of horridness concerning little girls.

Morris, flying high above the treetops, had a bird's eye view of everything. He chuckled as he watched Miss Gargoyle lumbering off along the wrong track. All the more time for Polly and the aunts to undo the spell, he thought.

Zigzagging along another path were Aunt Kitty and Aunt Winifred. They had dug out their old tandem bicycle which they were riding energetically, though not very skilfully. In their haste they crossed lawns and even flowerbeds, not caring for once about their precious plants.

Lastly, on yet another track, came Aunt Constance and Polly, and they were fast catching up.

Aunt Constance had proved herself to be even more resourceful and eccentric than Polly had first imagined. As soon as she had got outside, she had looked around for a means of transport. Seeing the messenger boy standing gossiping with a pot boy, she had snatched his scooter from him and, with hardly a word of explanation, leapt astride it.

'Shan't be long!' she told him. 'Jump on, Polly.'

'Do you know how to drive this?' Polly asked as she climbed rather nervously on to the back seat.

'Certainly,' said Aunt Constance, kicking the side of the machine and revving the engine. The scooter hiccupped with a bang and leapt backwards. Then, with a strong smell of burning rubber, it raced off with a roar across the lawn.

Polly wrapped her arms around her aunt, then she closed her eyes: perhaps it wouldn't be too bad if she couldn't see what they were likely to crash into.

Aunt Kitty and Aunt Winifred were the first to reach the topiary garden, or at least they thought they were, but actually Morris was there before them.

'I hardly dare look,' said Aunt Kitty, as she leaned the bicycle against the hedge. 'I don't think I can bear to see my poor boys like this.'

'Nonsense,' said Aunt Winifred, briskly. 'We'll soon have them out of here. Come on, there are so many bushes it could take some time to find them.'

'And when we do find them,' whimpered Aunt Kitty, peering at a neatly trimmed cockerel, 'what then? It's not as if we can undo the spell or anything.'

'We can guard them from that wicked Miss Gargoyle, though,' said Aunt Winifred. 'Better than nothing.'

It didn't take them long to discover the three green figures. Morris was already keeping watch from Uncle Fred's head, and he called out a welcoming 'Yark, yark,' as they approached.

'That's Polly's funny foreign bird,' said Winifred. 'Oh, and look, there they are!'

'Oh, the poor dears,' cried Aunt Kitty. 'Little Harry! Just look at him! What a sight, all twiggy and leaves instead of hair – oh, I can't bear it!'

'Nonsense,' said Aunt Winifred, sternly. 'We can't give in to hysterics now!' But her eyes glistened with tears too, and for a moment all she could do was stand and stare.

They were shaken out of their daze by the sudden loud hum of the motor scooter and, ten seconds later, Polly and Aunt Constance appeared.

'Constance! Goodness, where did the scooter come from? Are you both all right?' asked Aunt

Kitty. 'You haven't been out . . . It's the first time for so long . . .'

'I like a bit of an adventure,' said Aunt Constance. 'And I've been shut up there too long. Why didn't you tell me Miss Gargoyle was trying to make you hand over the rose in exchange for Fred and Tom?'

'We did,' said Aunt Winifred.

'Did you? Oh . . .' Aunt Constance looked surprised. 'I must have forgotten.' She peered at the green statues. 'And these are they? Are you sure? I mean, aren't they just bushes?'

'No,' said Polly. 'Harry found his father's pipe on that one and, well . . .' She didn't want to explain exactly how poor Harry had been tricked into drinking the magic potion. 'What else could they be?'

'Yes, they have to be them really, don't they? Extremely unfortunate for them.'

'But what on earth can we do?' said Aunt Kitty. 'That woman will be here at any moment.'

'Right. Now, what about the spell? Where is this famous little spell book?'

'I've got it,' said Winifred. 'But we can't make any sense of it. Look at the writing . . .'

Aunt Constance took the little book and opened it. She leafed through the pages quickly, peering at the strange letters, and after a few minutes began to chuckle.

'I'm sure Aunt Constance will be able to read it,' said Polly. 'She's just got to!'

'Quite right, Polly. Quite right,' she said. 'I *can* read this.' She giggled again.

'Constance! I really can't see anything amusing . . .' began Aunt Kitty. 'Just because they're not *your* husbands!'

'But you silly girls,' said Aunt Constance. 'Didn't you recognize it? Didn't you learn anything at school? This is shorthand! Just shorthand writing like any secretary would use.'

'What?' cried Kitty.

'What?' cried Winifred. She looked away crossly. 'Well, of course, *I* never did secretarial work . . .'

'A pity, is all I can say,' said Aunt Constance. 'Now, let's see. You think it's the one on page twenty-one, do you, Polly?'

'Yes,' said Polly. 'But when Miss Gargoyle did it she used some Super Fertilizer too, and made Harry drink it.'

'Oh, well, let's just hope we don't need any such things to undo it.' She studied the writing for several minutes while Kitty and Winifred shuffled their feet anxiously.

'Do hurry!' said Aunt Kitty.

'There are two bits,' said Aunt Constance, calmly, 'both rhymes, and this one seems to be the undoing one. Ready? All right. Here we go!

'You topiary figures on the lawn,
Have altered shape since you were born:
Now statue-like in earth you stand,
Your twiggy arms without a hand,
Legs are branches; grass-green eyes,
Rooted toes and trunk-like thighs.
Now, stick and leaf and bud-like posies,
Change into limbs and hair and noses!
From bushy prison – come! Escape!
Once more return to HUMAN SHAPE!'

As soon as Aunt Constance had spoken the final words, the three green figures began to twitch and rustle. It was as if a strong wind had suddenly sprung up inside them and was itching and pulling at their leaves. A few seconds later, the whole bush seemed to come alive as the leaves fell away, the bark peeled off, and suddenly arms and legs became separate, revealing the real person beneath.

Harry was the first to shake off all his leaves. 'Mother!' he cried, falling into her arms and

hugging her. 'That was awful. Do you know, I could see you all the time and hear you, but it was like looking through green glasses underwater. Horrible. And so frustrating. I wanted to shout out to you and couldn't!'

'Never mind. I'm just so glad to have you back, dear,' said Aunt Kitty. 'And look, here's your father.'

Within a few minutes, all three figures were returned to their proper state, and there was much rejoicing.

'But how did she get you under her spell?' asked Aunt Winifred, when the first greetings were all out of the way. 'That's what I simply can't understand.'

Uncle Fred looked sheepish and muttered something under his breath. He turned to Tom for support, but he was looking uncomfortable too.

'Well, um,' he began.

'Probably the same as with me,' said Harry. 'Miss Gargoyle tricked me and forced me to drink some beastly concoction she'd made. Honestly, she was so strong, like a wild animal, and the things she said . . . she must have been weaving some terrible magic on me all the time I was there!'

'It was very brave of you to go there at all,' said Aunt Kitty, fondly.

Morris and Polly exchanged a meaningful look.

'Yes, wasn't it,' said Polly in a cold voice. 'And I suppose, if only she hadn't tied you to the table and held your mouth open with red-hot pincers while she poured this dreadful concoction in, you'd have been able to overpower her?'

'Well, er,' said Harry, blushing. 'Something like that, anyway. Of course you weren't there, so you can't imagine how awful it all was, but . . .'

'Don't worry,' said Polly. 'I've got a very good imagination, thanks!'

'Sounds very much like how it happened to us, Harry,' said his father. 'A very tricky woman that Miss Gargoyle. Very tricky!'

'Anyway,' said Aunt Winifred, 'the family is reunited once more so let's not worry too much about how it all happened.'

'Quite,' said Aunt Constance. 'Now that's settled, all we have to do is sort out Miss Gargoyle!'

Chapter Thirteen

The reunited family settled comfortably in the kitchen to talk about the events of the past few days over a cup of tea and some chocolate cake.

'I'm very grateful to you, Polly dear,' said Uncle Tom. 'It was very clever of you to find us and very brave of you to confront Miss Gargoyle like that.'

'Hear, hear,' said Uncle Fred. 'And might I add how delighted I am to meet you at last, Polly. It's been far too long since we saw Edward, and so silly of us to let this blue rose business come between us.'

'Do explain,' said Polly, blushing madly and eager to change the subject. 'I've been wanting to know ever since I came . . . Did my father grow a blue rose and then take it away? Is that it?'

'Not exactly,' said Aunt Constance. 'He hadn't completed it. We wanted him to stay and work on it, but, by then, he'd fallen in love with your mother who was an enthusiastic ornithologist - bird-lover to you, Harry - and that's what he wanted to do too. I think Miss Gargoyle rather fell in love with him, or maybe just with the blue rose he talked about and she never forgot it. Years later, when she saw our advertisement for a gardener, she came, hoping to get her hands on the rose again.'

'Of course, we should never have employed her. It was only because she'd known your father,' said Aunt Kitty.

'But what about that blue rose he was working on?' Polly asked again.

'Oh, it was silly. We had a dreadful row because he wouldn't stay and he took it with him, along with all his notes and everything.'

Polly's brain was spinning and her thoughts were a jumble, but somewhere, at the back of her mind, she thought she might have the beginnings of an answer.

'What about this Miss Gargoyle, then?' said Aunt Winifred. 'That's what we really must think about now.'

'She'll be back,' said Uncle Fred. 'You mark my words, that woman, witch, whatever she is, she'll be back.'

'You're right,' said Aunt Winifred.

'So what are we going to do?'

'Give her the rose?' suggested Aunt Kitty. 'I mean, she's not going to stop, is she, not until she's got it.'

'You can't,' said Polly. 'It's yours.'

'We can grow another . . . I suppose . . . in twenty years or so . . .'

'It's not even very blue yet,' said Aunt Constance. 'She won't like it. She won't believe it's real.'

'Then we must give her one she *can* believe,' said Uncle Tom, with a mischievous grin.

'What do you mean?'

'I don't know quite, just an idea. There must be something . . .'

Just then, the back door flew open with a bang. Everyone started and turned to the doorway.

Miss Gargoyle stood there, her magnificent plaits now drooping in long swathes and loops around her shoulders, her overalls torn and dirty. The shears were still in her hand, but she no longer had the strength to brandish them. Her cheeks were pale and her eyes strangely bright.

She glared round the room at them.

'Very cosy,' she snarled. 'What a pretty picture! Everybody happy now? Got them back,

147

eh? Patting yourselves on the back over a nice cup of tea? Hah!'

She took a step into the kitchen, giving her shears an experimental, but not very convincing, snap.

'I suppose you think I'm finished now, don't you? Suppose you hoity-toity ladies think you've won? Well, you haven't!'

'Please, Miss Gargoyle,' said Aunt Kitty, gently. 'Please, control yourself.'

'I will not!' said the witch. 'I don't want to! I shan't!'

'What do you want, Miss Gargoyle?' asked Uncle Fred, standing up. 'How can we help?'

'Stop being so lah-di-dah!' screeched the witch. 'I'm through with politeness. I'm through with games. I want that rose!'

'There isn't a blue rose,' said Aunt Constance. 'Edward never finished it.'

'I don't believe you,' said Miss Gargoyle sharply, trying to stop the doubt creeping into her voice. 'There is.'

'I assure you there isn't,' said Aunt Constance.

'There is! There is!' said the witch, stamping her feet. 'Up in that greenhouse. I haven't finished yet. I'll get it! I'll have it yet!' She glared round at the faces challengingly. 'I shall get it,' she said, more gently now. 'I shall. You may have won for the moment, but I don't give up that easily. That rose was meant to be mine. It belongs to me.'

Then she spun round and marched out again.

'Phew!' said Harry.

'There we are,' said Uncle Tom, 'just as we thought. She won't stop until she gets it.'

'Shall I just go and get it then?' suggested Aunt Kitty, again. 'I mean, is it worth all this . . .?'

'Certainly not!' snapped Aunt Winifred. 'Not after we've come so far. Besides, I don't think we shall have to . . . What did you mean, Tom, when you said a rose she'd believe?'

'Why, I was just thinking,' said Uncle Tom, smiling, 'that since we really *don't* have a very blue rose, and certainly not the blue rose she wants, and Miss Gargoyle so desperately wants one, that we should make her one.'

'How?' said Harry. 'I thought that was what Aunt Constance had been trying to do all these years.'

'Oh, I know, I know!' cried Polly. 'Like we did at school; we used to dye carnations and things with ink. We could do that!'

'Yes, Polly,' said Uncle Tom. 'That's the idea, something like that. Only we'll have to make it really good, exactly like the real thing. And then we'll have to set a trap. The more difficult it is for her to get, the more pleased she'll be when she gets it.'

The first problem was to make a blue rose.

Using ink the way Polly suggested didn't work; it took too long. But then Aunt Constance and Aunt Kitty thought of paint. They had several white roses with which to experiment and they tried all the blue paint they had in the house. None of them looked real, they simply coated the petals with a thick, unnatural layer. Then Aunt Constance thought of her blue hair rinse: it was coloured, but not thick. They mixed it up as directed on the packet and then very carefully applied it to the petals. It worked. The dye was just strong enough to be absorbed by the white petals without looking as though it was painted on. The subtle silvery–blue looked both natural and attractive.

'It looks wonderful,' said Aunt Kitty, wist–

fully. 'Even I could imagine it was the real thing
. . .'

'But won't she realize?' asked Polly. 'Won't
she be suspicious?'

'Why should she be?' asked Harry. 'She wants
a blue rose. She believes there is one, and this
is it!'

When they were quite happy with the appearance of the new blue flower, they had to decide
what to do with it.

'We won't hide it,' said Uncle Tom, 'we'll just
put it back in the greenhouse, otherwise she'll
suspect we're trying to trick her.'

'Do you really think she'll come and look for
it?' asked Aunt Kitty.

'I'm sure she will. Either with the help of her
awful magic or without it.'

'But won't she be suspicious if we just leave it
there?' asked Polly.

'Not if we lock it up and lock up the house,'
said Aunt Winifred.

'I think you're right,' agreed Aunt Constance.

So they spent the rest of the evening setting
their plan in motion.

First they put up a giant spotlight to shine on
to the greenhouse: it would stay alight all night
long and nobody could creep up without being

on view. Then they arranged trip wires and alarm bells all round it and around the house.

By the time it was dark, all was ready. The new blue rose had been substituted for the old pale blue one, which was hidden somewhere else in the house. The blue rose's pot was chained to the floor of the greenhouse, and the greenhouse itself was locked and double locked.

'Crikey!' said Harry. 'I don't know how she's going to get through this lot!'

'She will, don't you worry,' said Uncle Tom. 'If she wants this rose badly enough, she will.'

Chapter Fourteen

Night fell. The moon cast silvery shadows across the lawns and all was quiet.

Harry, Morris and Polly were not asleep. Crouching at a window which overlooked the front of the house and the rooftop greenhouse, they watched and waited.

'D'you think she'll come tonight?'

'I bet she can't wait a minute longer,' said Harry. 'Crikey! Look down there, can you see something?'

They leaned forward and peered down into the gloom.

The spotlight on the roof was bright but its rays hardly illuminated the walls of the house and only faintly lit the ground around. The shadows were black and deep.

'Something's moving down there,' hissed Polly. 'Yes, I saw something.'

'It's her! It's her!' Harry whispered loudly. 'Look!'

Miss Gargoyle was creeping stealthily towards the house.

She had already circled it once, looking for anything out of the ordinary, and now she was certain the rose was up in the greenhouse on the roof. Why else would they have lit it up like that? Huh, that wouldn't stop her!

She was carrying a rake and a large bag which she now put down on the ground beside her. Leaning back, she gazed up at the towering wall in front of her. The light shone down on her and lit her face up: white and shadowy, it looked like a mask. She smiled broadly and the mask cracked, elongating her nose and eyes; she looked more sinister than ever, and just like a witch.

Then, lifting her arms up to her head, she began to undo her hair.

'What's she doing?' asked Polly in amazement, as Miss Gargoyle began, one by one, to remove the pins and clips which fastened the strange hairstyle in place.

'She's doing her hair,' whispered Harry. 'Crikey, why's she doing her hair at this time of night?'

As the pins were removed, the masses of hair fell down in great coils on the earth beside her, lying like ropes on the deck of a ship. More and more hair slithered to the ground until it was all undone and there was just one long plait hanging from her head to the pile on the floor.

'Rapunzel,' squeaked Morris softly into Polly's ear.

'What's that?' said Harry, puzzled.

'Rapunzel,' Polly said, more loudly. 'She's like Rapunzel in the fairy story.'

They watched incredulously as Miss Gargoyle sorted out the great tangle of hair. When it was neatly on the floor, and Miss Gargoyle had hold of the free end, she bent down and took something from her bag. It was something which moved. Something with wings.

'I can't see,' said Harry. 'I can't see. What is it?'

'Her bats!' said Polly. 'It's those bats. Yuk!'

Miss Gargoyle took out two bats and, by tying their feet to her hair, attached them to the end of her plait. Next, with a mighty heave, she threw them up towards the roof.

The bats fluttered their wings, flapped wildly, and then rose jerkily towards the roof carrying the long, long plait of hair with them.

As soon as they reached the flat roof outside

Aunt Constance's room, the bats circled around looking for a suitable place to rest. At last they chose some protruding guttering pipe and, with a few more flaps of their wings, they wound the end of the rope round the pipe. When it was tightly fixed, they stopped and, hanging upside down from beneath the gutter, seemed to go to sleep.

'Rapunzel, Rapunzel, let UP your hair!' cried Polly. 'She's going to climb it!'

'Yark,' agreed Morris.

Polly was right. Once her hair was secure, Miss Gargoyle gave it a few tugs. It seemed to satisfy her, for then, slinging her bag over her shoulder, the rake pushed inside it, she began to climb.

Despite her shape and weight, she was surprisingly agile, and bracing herself squarely against the bricks she began to walk slowly up the wall. The ivies and flowers didn't seem to hamper her progress and, in only a short time, she had scaled the wall and was clambering over the rim of the roof.

'So much for the alarm bells on the back and front door and all the locks on all the windows,' said Harry.

'Shh! Look! What's she doing now?'

'You'd think she'd put that light out.'

'Not her!' said Polly. 'I bet she knows we're watching. I bet she'd like everyone to see!'

As if Miss Gargoyle had heard them, she turned and waved triumphantly into the dark.

Next, Miss Gargoyle folded up her hair neatly so it lay in coils along the rooftop. When she had finished, she turned to the greenhouse, rubbing her hands together gleefully.

'This is going to be more difficult,' said Harry. 'If she smashes the glass, all the alarm bells will go off and that'll bring Dad and Uncle Fred.'

'But they want her to get the rose,' said Polly.

'Oh, yes, but it wouldn't do to let it look *too* easy!'

Miss Gargoyle circled the greenhouse several times. She studied the door but didn't touch the many locks and chains which held it fast.

'What's she going to do?'

Miss Gargoyle had opened her bag again and was groping around inside it. Eventually she brought out two objects. One was about the size of a large currant bun, and the other was much smaller. They couldn't see what either one was until the witch turned back into the light, and the children saw that the larger of the objects was a toad. Its characteristic shape showed up sharply against the light: thick, short arms sticking out in front and long back legs dangling behind.

'What on earth does she want . . .?'

'Shh!'

Miss Gargoyle stepped back from the greenhouse and, raising her arm, seemed to throw the poor animal against it. There was a soft 'splat' noise and the toad stuck against the glass, the strong suction pads on its toes holding firmly to the smooth surface. Quickly the witch set to work with the other tool she had brought, a glass cutter, cutting the pane around the animal.

'Clever!' cried Harry. 'She's using him like a handle.'

Some strange chortles and wheezes coming from Morris meant he thought it was funny as well as clever.

'Is that bird all right?' asked Harry.

'Fine, fine,' said Polly. 'Shh, look.'

As Miss Gargoyle cut out the pane of glass, she kept hold of the toad, so that when she had quite finished, all she had to do was lift out the sheet of glass using the toad as a handle. There was no noise and no mess and no alarm bells went off.

Miss Gargoyle had almost finished, she was just seconds away from her goal, when there was a shout and Uncle Fred and Aunt Winifred burst through a little door from one of the towers alongside.

'Stop!' cried Aunt Winifred. 'That's ours!'

Polly and Harry stiffened in alarm. Why were they interfering?

'Why . . .?' Harry managed to say.

'They're just pretending,' said Polly, suddenly realizing. 'Making it look more real.'

'I hope you're right.'

Miss Gargoyle had turned sharply when the two people arrived on the scene, but she didn't seem perturbed.

'What is?' said Miss Gargoyle. 'Something bothering you? Can't a body pay a visit without being shouted at? Something special about this greenhouse? This roof?'

'The rose!' cried Aunt Winifred.

'But there isn't any rose,' said Miss Gargoyle. 'You told me so yourself. Don't come any closer,' she warned as Uncle Fred took a step forward.

'Hah hum,' said Uncle Fred, twiddling his moustache as if he was very nervous. 'Don't touch that plant,' he added unconvincingly.

Miss Gargoyle sneered.

'Pooh!' she said. 'You're nothing!' And she stooped down suddenly and drew yet another object from her bag. This time it happened too quickly for anyone to see; one minute her hand was in the bag, the next, in one fluid movement, she was pulling out a vast thin net.

At first Polly thought it was tissue paper or gauze, then she recognized it. It was an enormous spider's web.

Miss Gargoyle flung the web across the roof: it hung suspended in the air above Aunt Winifred and Uncle Fred for a second and then fell like a silver cloud, enveloping them in a haze of sticky, clinging strands.

The captives struggled briefly then sank on to the floor. It was hopeless. With every move they made, the net just grew tighter and more gummy.

'Miss Clever Cloggsy Poggsy what's-her-name may have my spell book,' said the witch, 'but I've still got my menagerie!'

She turned back to the greenhouse and quickly put her hand in through the hole she'd made. The rose was right in the middle of the greenhouse. No ordinary person would have reached it, but with a sly grin on her face, Miss Gargoyle began to stretch her arm: longer and longer it grew, until her plump fingers at last touched the rose petals. She fingered it briefly, then, quickly, ignoring the chain around the plant pot, she simply lifted the blue rose from its pot, roots and all, and pulled it out.

'At last!' she cried. 'At last. It's my rose, my blue rose.' She gazed down at it fondly. 'So I win, don't I? Eh? I knew I would. You can't stop me when I'm on form. I've stumped you now, haven't I?'

'Yes, you've got it,' said Aunt Winifred from under the cloak of cobweb. 'You've won. That's the only blue rose in the world and probably the last.'

Aunt Constance appeared suddenly from her bedroom doorway.

'Oh, Miss Gargoyle,' she said calmly, 'you've got it.'

'Absolutely,' said the witch. 'And it's really lovely.'

'I'm not going to try and stop you,' said Aunt Constance, seeing the plight of the other two beneath the net, 'but just do listen.'

'Well?'

'We haven't finished all the tests yet. We're certainly not at a stage where we would exhibit this rose. It really needs years more research . . .'

'Huh, you're just making it up . . .'

'No, really, it fades. It changes colour. The leaves drop off. There are so many problems.'

'Lies. Lies. You want it for yourself. My Edward wouldn't have made a blue rose that faded. Anyway, enough chit-chat, I didn't come to pass the time of day – sorry – night with you. I'm off.' She hugged the rose to her chest and smiled. 'But this won't be the last you'll hear of me. Oh, won't you be jealous when you see my name in all the papers? Me and the rose'll be on the news too, pictures and everything, and at the Chelsea Flower Show and oh, everywhere. I'm going to call it "Gertie's Blue Wonder" . . .'

She sighed happily. 'Right then. That's that. I'm off.'

'Just a minute,' cried Aunt Winifred. 'What about us?'

'What about you?'

'Can't you take this, this thing off?' cried Uncle Fred.

Miss Gargoyle was busily packing her bag, carefully settling the rose in it and putting back the toad and glass cutter.

'Sorry,' she said, not even looking up. 'I can't. No spell book, remember. It's got a life of its own that book, I'm always losing it. Shan't need it for a while. It'll find its way back, it always does. Well, must get along. Bye!'

With a wide smile, she waved a hand at them in mock salute. Then, taking hold of her hair which still lay in thin coils on the roof, she began to bundle it into her arms. In a few moments she had picked it all up and the two bats were fluttering in the air above her head with the end in their claws. Then she picked up her rake and settled herself astride it.

'Farewell!' she cried, leaping off the roof into the black void below. 'FAREWELL . . .'

'It's a broomstick!' cried Harry, as the rake shot out into the sky.

'It's a rakestick!' said Polly. 'And it doesn't work very well.'

The bats flapped and fluttered. For a few moments they and the rake supported Miss Gargoyle, but then, as if there wasn't enough magic, or she was just too fat, Miss Gargoyle plunged downwards.

By the time Aunt Constance had reached the edge and was peering over, the witch and her belongings had reached the ground – somewhat faster than any of them had intended.

Polly and Harry stared down: Miss Gargoyle wasn't hurt. She dusted herself down, scooped up her mass of hair and stuffed it into her bag, then, pausing only to shake her rake crossly, disappeared into the blackness of the surrounding bushes.

Chapter Fifteen

Polly and Harry were too far away to hear much of the conversation on the roof, but they had seen everything and as soon as Miss Gargoyle had disappeared, they made their way to Aunt Constance's room.

Morris was wheezing and chortling in an alarming manner, but he assured Polly, when no one was looking, that he was quite well, just thoroughly amused.

Everyone gathered in Aunt Constance's blue room. The aunts and uncles were still in their nightwear; they hadn't had a chance to change before they found the witch had come.

'Well, she fell for it all right,' Uncle Tom was saying as they arrived. He lit his pipe and settled down on the blue and white striped sofa. 'Better than we thought.'

'Put that dreadful pipe out and come and help

me with Winifred and Fred,' said Aunt Kitty. 'They're all tangled up.'

'Oh, hello, you two,' said Uncle Tom, seeing Polly and Harry. 'She believed us. She's taken the fake rose.'

'We saw,' said Polly. 'Is everyone all right?'

'Come and help get this blasted net off!' cried Uncle Fred from outside.

It took a long time to untangle Aunt Winifred and Uncle Fred from the sticky web. It clung to their hair and clothes like glue, but at last they were free from most of it, and then they all went downstairs and opened a bottle of sparkling parsnip wine which was one of Uncle Fred's specialities. Everyone had a glass to celebrate.

'Thank goodness she didn't have that spell book with her,' said Aunt Winifred. 'She was quite powerful enough without it.'

'Yes, what did happen to it anyway?' said Aunt Kitty, looking round as if she expected it to appear suddenly. 'You had it last, Constance.'

'Did I? I suppose I must have done.'

'I didn't see where you put it,' said Polly. 'Did you put it down? Perhaps it evaporated or something magical like that.'

'Who knows?' said Aunt Winifred. 'But I think it's good riddance to bad rubbish, as they say.'

'So do I,' agreed Uncle Fred. 'It obviously hampered her power with that old rake too. Good Lord, wish I could fly around the place on a hoe or something. Save me a lot of legwork!'

While they drank the bubbling wine, they went over the events of the night, the grown-ups telling the children what Miss Gargoyle had said, since they hadn't been able to hear from where they'd been watching.

'So she really does believe it's a blue rose,' said Harry. 'At least, she does now. But what happens when she finds out it isn't?'

'I don't know,' said Aunt Kitty. 'But I bet she'll be furious.'

'I hope she doesn't come back,' said Harry.

'I have a feeling,' said Aunt Kitty, 'that she has no intention of taking that rose anywhere, not to Chelsea or the Rose Appreciation Society or anywhere. She's the sort of person who would just want it for herself.'

'You mean she'll just sit and look at it?' asked Polly.

'Yes. And when the colour doesn't last, perhaps she'll believe what Constance said.'

'Don't know why she didn't just magic herself one,' said Harry. 'I would have.'

'Yes, you would,' agreed his father. 'But even

witches have scruples.'

'What are those?'

'Oh *Harry!*'

'If only your father had gone on with his research, Polly,' said Aunt Constance, wistfully. 'He was so near . . .'

'Oh, golly!' Polly cried, suddenly. 'I've just had the most tremendous thought!'

Without another word, Polly jumped off her chair and ran upstairs. She hurried up the spiral staircase to her room and flung open the balcony windows. She just had to see that plant of her father's!

When she had left it earlier, the buds had been just about to open and now, just as she hoped, they had . . . the plant had bloomed!

She brought it into the light. Yes! It was just as she had begun to suspect. She smiled: Wonderful! Wonderful! She picked it up quickly and sped downstairs again as fast as she could.

'Here you are!' she cried, rushing back into the room where everyone was. 'Just look at this! It's from my father. A present. He said not to give it to you until it flowered. I couldn't think why, but now I know.'

And she handed Aunt Constance a rose whose petals were as blue as the sky on a summer's day.

'Oh, my goodness me!' cried Aunt Constance.

'How glorious!' said Aunt Kitty.

'Magnificent!' said Uncle Tom.

'Stupendous!' said Aunt Winifred.

'Jolly good show!' said Uncle Fred.

'Cultivated cauliflowers!' said Harry. 'It's the real thing!'

Aunt Constance's eyes filled with tears as she reached out trembling hands to take it.

'Would you believe the beauty of it! The shape of those petals! The scent – a perfect aroma! The blueness!'

171

'It's exquisite,' agreed Aunt Winifred, examining it. 'And not only just blue, but striped with darker veins and such a lovely design!'

'We have our own blue rose at last,' said Aunt Constance. 'Oh, dear Edward. Dear, clever Edward.'

'It's grand,' said Uncle Fred, 'but you realize we'll never be able to show it. Or not for a long time. Soon as Miss Gargoyle sees it she'll know we cheated her.'

'Then we won't,' said Aunt Constance quietly. 'We'll just keep it here for us. For us to appreciate and love.'

Morris pecked gently at Polly's ear. He had kept very quiet while everyone was around and was bursting to speak.

'Fuss and bother,' he whispered. 'Roses are meant to be red. Has it got any tasty caterpillars on it, that's what I'd like to know.'

While the adults were exclaiming over the beauty of the rose, examining its petals and leaves, Harry wandered across the room to Polly.

'Guess what I've got,' he said in a low voice.

'What?'

'Look!' And he pulled out the witch's spell book from beneath his jumper.

Morris squawked loudly.

Polly opened her mouth to protest, but Harry interrupted.

'Shh! Don't tell them,' he said, pushing the book quickly out of sight. 'But, hey, Polly, don't you think we'll be able to have some fun with it?'

'No. I'm not sure you should have it at all, Harry,' Polly said. 'It's not yours and it could be dangerous.'

'Don't be so wet! You sound worse than them!' he said, indicating his parents. 'But you won't tell, will you?'

Morris made a 'yark' noise which sounded very like a 'yes'.

'Crikey! What a noise. Can't you shut that parrot up?'

Morris fluffed his feathers up crossly and squawked.

'He's a macaw, actually,' said Polly.

'What's the difference? Anyway, doesn't he do anything except make that revolting noise all the time or frighten people? Does he do tricks? I bet he could be fun to play with. Why do you keep him all to yourself?'

'He doesn't like boys,' said Polly. 'He can be a bit dangerous with boys.'

'He doesn't look dangerous.'

'Appearances can be very deceptive,' said Polly, sweetly. 'And believe me, they wouldn't call him Monster Morris the Male-Mangling Macaw for nothing, you know.'

Morris turned to Polly, cocking his head, his beady eyes round with surprise. He opened his beak and for a moment Polly thought he was going to break his vow and speak, but instead he began to make the most TERRIBLE noise. It was like rusty iron grating down blackboards, like sandpaper scratching against rough glass, like a hyena stuck down a deep hole.

Everyone turned towards him in alarm.

'Is he all right?' asked Uncle Tom. 'What a ghastly row. Is he having a fit?'

'Oh, no,' said Polly smiling. 'He's perfectly all right. He's just laughing. Don't worry, he doesn't do it very often, I promise.'

Everyone was very, very relieved to hear it.

THE END

If you would like to receive a Newsletter about our new Children's books, just fill in the coupon below with your name and address (or copy it onto a separate piece of paper if you don't want to spoil your book) and send it to:

The Children's Books Editor
Transworld Publishers Ltd.
61–63 Uxbridge Road
Ealing
London W5 5SA

Please send me a Children's Newsletter:

Name: ....

Address: ....

....

....

All Children's Books are available at your bookshop or newsagent, or can be ordered from the following address:
Transworld Publishers Ltd.
Cash Sales Department,
P.O. Box 11, Falmouth, Cornwall TR10 9EN

UK and B.F.P.O. customers please send a cheque or postal order (no currency) and allow £1.00 for postage and packing for the first book plus 50p for the second book and 30p for each additional book to a maximum charge of £3.00 (7 books plus).

Overseas customers, including Eire, please allow £2.00 for postage and packing for the first book plus £1.00 for the second book and 50p for each subsequent title ordered.